Logan opened the car door. The ache in his chest refused to ease and continued to grow and intensify. Damn emotions. Why couldn't they just stay stuffed down where he'd shoved them?

His eyes shifted to the shop building, his gaze drawn toward the large window and the woman standing inside. A strange, unfamiliar tingling surfaced from the deep recess of his stomach, slowly prickling and twisting through his whole body.

Staring harder at the woman, he took in her appearance, slowly moving over the mustard-yellow top she was wearing to rest on her long blond hair and strong features. She looked familiar. Like someone he once briefly knew. A woman who'd tempted him to do unfamiliar and sinful things he'd never tried before. Someone whose gorgeous body he'd explored intimately during one long night.

Someone whose sweet, kissable and frankly too-enticing mouth he still dreamed about all these months later…

Dear Reader,

Thank you for choosing to spend time with *Reunited by Her Twin Revelation*.

Have you ever had a revelation knock your world into an alarming spin? Well, Dr. Logan Fox is about to find out exactly how that feels when he discovers that family sometimes comes in small baby bundles—times two!

Being thrust into his new father role also means coming into daily contact with nurse Thurza Bow, his sons' far-too-lovely mother and the woman he can't stop thinking about.

I hope you enjoy Logan and Thurza's journey.

Best wishes,

Shelley xxx

REUNITED BY HER TWIN REVELATION

SHELLEY RIVERS

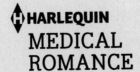

MEDICAL
ROMANCE

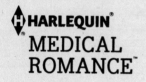

HARLEQUIN®
MEDICAL
ROMANCE™

Recycling programs
for this product may
not exist in your area.

ISBN-13: 978-1-335-40886-0

Reunited by Her Twin Revelation

Copyright © 2021 by Shelley Rivers

This edition published by arrangement with Harlequin Books S.A.

For questions and comments about the quality of this book, please contact us at CustomerService@Harlequin.com.

Harlequin Enterprises ULC
22 Adelaide St. West, 40th Floor
Toronto, Ontario M5H 4E3, Canada
www.Harlequin.com

Printed in U.S.A.

Shelley Rivers is a Bournemouth girl who spent most of her childhood reading. Married with a family, she now splits most of her time between reading, writing and pandering to the whims of her hilarious greyhound. Her hobbies include lopsided sewing, holey knitting and collecting old stuff that no one else sees the beauty in.

Books by Shelley Rivers

Harlequin Medical Romance

Tempted by the Brooding Vet
Awakening His Shy Vet

Visit the Author Profile page at Harlequin.com.

To C, with love.

A special thanks to paramedic Graham Woolcott for his expert help during the writing of this story.

**Praise for
Shelley Rivers**

CHAPTER ONE

'SO YOU ARE really leaving us?'

Dr Logan Fox glanced up from studying the computer screen and smiled at the old man waiting his turn in the busy waiting room. Several small children sat reading books on the tiled floor, and a group of mothers stood beside the small babies' play area at the far end of the room, whispering and laughing as they waited to be called for their appointments.

With a smile of thanks to the receptionist, Logan wove his way over to the local man who'd become a good friend during his months while working on the island of Malta. The man who had helped him through many a long, lonely night, as they jointly put the world to rights in the crowded surroundings of a local bar.

'I am indeed, Matthew. In less than two hours I shall be on a plane to England. My taxi is due to arrive within the hour to take me to the airport.'

'Have we driven you away with all our sunshine and steep, narrow streets?' the old man joked, shooting Logan a toothy grin. His left hand clutched a brown wooden walking stick—a stick it had taken Logan weeks to convince him to use.

Logan smiled and shook his head. 'No, it's time I went home and tied up the last of my father's estate. Retrieved the few belongings I wish to keep before the house and everything inside it is sold. I've put it off long enough, but the solicitors are threatening to send over a team of mercenaries to kidnap me and take me back to England if I don't return this coming week. Worse still, they insist they'll charge me for the trouble.'

Matthew chuckled, the deep, strong sound at odds with the man's small and wizened stature. Logan had learnt while treating his friend after his last health scare that he had great stamina, and his mind was as strong and as sharp as a teenager's—and just as crafty.

'Well, just make sure you come back to us,' Matthew insisted. 'Old Doc isn't going to last much longer. I swear the man was ancient when I was a boy, running through the countryside with nothing but merriment and mischief on my mind.'

Logan chuckled. 'Between you and me, I think the man intends to continue working until the next millennium. Anyway, you'll be far too busy to miss me as I hear you're looking for another wife. Though surely five is enough for any man's lifetime?'

Matthew tutted and removed his cream Havana hat. 'Any man who is tired of women should be rotting in the grave, my dear friend. Is it my fault that women keep leaving me? Inconvenient, it is. You just get used to one and then she either ruins things by croaking it or she runs off. Besides, I'm still looking for *her*.'

'Her?' Logan repeated curiously.

'Yes—you know, the special one. The one who is supposed to fill your heart with everything your soul requires. I've come close with each of my wives, but never quite got it right. Good, but not perfect.'

'Then why marry at all?' Logan quizzed the man, who had a reputation in town for being a long-time rogue and charmer.

Matthew grinned again, and this time a rakish twinkle lit up his ageing eyes. 'A man has to pass the time somehow while he's waiting for "the one", Logan. It can get lonely and boring otherwise. And kissing the wrong women has many, many sweet advantages.'

Logan laughed and patted his friend on the shoulder. 'I guess you're right.'

With a final farewell, Logan left the building and stepped out on to the old narrow street. Passing small bars and tiny shops crammed full of goods to buy, he walked the short distance to the traditional Maltese house he shared with a male nurse from the same health practice. With luck he would have the place to himself while he finished packing his suitcase. He and the other members of staff had said their goodbyes the night before, when they'd all shared a meal and several bottles of the local wine at Old Doc's house. Now he just wanted to slip away without any fuss.

Strolling down a second narrow street, he continued on until he came to a small courtyard concealed from the main busy thoroughfare. Built from the local limestone, three-storey buildings rose around Logan, cocooning him within their rough, golden weathered walls. Passing an open gate, he could smell freshly baked bread, garlic and the local culinary speciality of rabbit stew filling the air. With a glance inside he observed groups of locals and tourists, tucking into mouth-watering plates of food courtesy of the hidden backstreet restaurant.

Moving on, he ignored the tantalising and tempting aromas that called to his empty stomach and teased his appetite, disappointed not to have time to enjoy one last meal before leaving. But he'd made up his mind to travel today and it was too late to change his plans.

In the far corner of the courtyard a small child ran up a flight of stone steps, singing a nursery rhyme. Nearby, his doting grandmother sat on a stool, watching.

Logan waved to the old woman, but headed for the traditional blue arched door in the opposite corner. Purple tube-shaped flowers spilled down from the black wrought-iron balcony just above it, the sprawling lower leaves brushing the top of his head as he unlocked the door. The familiar sensation brought a moment of pleasure to his restless soul.

Letting himself into the building, he climbed the narrow steps to his bedroom, glad to reach it without encountering anyone. He just wanted to pack and leave. Say goodbye to the island the same way he'd arrived. Without fuss or fanfare. Malta had become his refuge after his failed engagement, and leaving it arose mixed feelings he refused to examine or dissect. If not for the solicitor's insistence that he return to England, he wouldn't be going home at all.

Entering his bedroom, Logan let his gaze fall immediately on the half-packed suitcase lying open on the double bed. Glancing around, he checked over the rest of the furniture for any remaining belongings, his eyes eventually landing on the folded letter on the dressing table.

It was a letter he'd spent the last few months ignoring, after discarding it there following one single read. He was refusing to deal with the reality of what lay folded inside the envelope and his feelings towards the people it concerned.

Reluctantly, he walked over to the dressing table and picked it up. A thin layer of dust now covered it. Blowing off the worst, he slowly turned it over, staring down at the thick paper, not eager to confront the strange jumble of emotions it triggered inside him.

The words printed within informed him of several facts he would have preferred never to discover. The main one being that Victor Fox, the man Logan had believed was his father, did not, in truth, share one particle of DNA with him.

Which meant that for thirty-five years every single person in Logan's so-called family had lied to him. Each one guilty of deception by choosing to keep the loathsome truth a secret.

Apparently everyone had known his mother's dirty little lie—except for him. The person it concerned the most. The individual who'd been fed a dishonest fairy tale, only to discover a sordid tangle of falsehoods.

Nausea rotated in Logan's stomach, but he ignored it and forced himself to list the uncomfortable truths mentally. His beloved late mother had indulged in a long-term love affair at some time during her twenty-year marriage to Victor. An affair which resulted in a child—him. Facts he'd only discovered after reading this letter from Victor's solicitor. Precise, impersonal words, disclosing the ugly facts and the information his so-called family had purposely chosen to keep from him. Telling him that Logan could use the Fox name, but that not one drop of genuine Fox blood flowed through his veins, making him null and void as the man's assumed son and heir.

Making Logan's presence in the family entirely irrelevant now Victor no longer lived.

The aching tightness in Logan's chest had nothing to do with the light cold he'd picked up a few days ago. No, the pain spreading out from the area around his heart originated from the callous reality that betrayal and treachery stained his whole existence. That, despite believing differently, Logan actually had no true family other than an estranged half-brother.

Was this destiny's sick joke? A way to knock him off his complacent perch and show him that trust was nothing but a foolish hope? Something people liked to offer and declare, but rarely executed for the benefit of others?

With each breath, the ache in Logan's chest increased. The constant thick tension that had begun the day news of Victor's death had reached him. News only forwarded after the man's funeral in England had already taken place. Exactly the way Victor had desired it, according to Bellman, his faithful solicitor.

No bedside farewells or last-minute explanations for him. Just these blunt and impersonal words on a piece of paper that shattered and destroyed everything Logan had thought true. An abrupt statement proclaiming his mother's adultery and Victor's swift and brutal renouncement of Logan as his true son. No other explanation or justification given.

One night he had gone to sleep a son but awoken the following day as no one.

Logan's fingers tightened around the letter. Everything he'd been raised to believe in had been harshly ripped away without care or thought for his feelings. Leaving him cast aside like one of Victor's flawed business deals. Cold-heartedly disconnected from the birthright he'd assumed was his to claim.

Who knew why Victor had chosen to reveal the truth after so many years pretending? The man's thought process had always at best bordered on complicated, so there was no point in trying to decipher this last action.

Victor's vast fortune would be distributed through various charities and associations. Gifts to good causes—another out-of-character act from the old man. Logan didn't need or care about the money, or the ridiculously large house in Salisbury where he'd grown up. None of the material possessions mattered—only the bitter truth that the man he'd always believed cared for him had mercilessly rejected any familial connection linking them once he no longer had use for Logan. Once he no longer required a son.

After years of sharing what Logan had believed was a strong, close father-and-son relationship, Victor had discarded both his affection and his presence in the family with soul-obliterating and ruthless ease.

All Logan's life Victor had drummed home

a mantra of discipline, hard work and family loyalty. He'd pushed Logan to be the best at everything and to reject failure. When Logan had gone to university Victor had chosen which one, and what career Logan would pursue. As he'd had a natural ability for science and excelled in tests, he'd decided on medicine. Not a general doctor, though. No, Victor had expected Logan to become the best in his field. Always the greatest. Because any less would be neither allowed nor contemplated.

Thankfully Logan had also wished to pursue medicine. He'd loved working with patients and finding ways to heal them, so there'd been no hardship in following Victor's wishes. Not when they had also been his own.

The only time Logan had witnessed the old man's anger and disappointment had occurred on the day he'd informed Victor that he planned to go to Malta, after calling off his six-month engagement to the daughter of a family friend. Then he'd seen something in Victor's eyes that had unsettled him. Some emotion that made sense to him now.

Tugging off his black-framed glasses, Logan tucked them into his shirt pocket and headed in the direction of the bed. Throwing the letter inside the suitcase, he reached for the lid, then paused. After a second's hesitation, he snatched the letter out again. With one final look, he scrunched it into a messy ball and walked over to the wastepaper bin. Dropping it inside, he glared at the crumpled letter for a moment longer before turning away.

He had no need to keep it when the words were already burnt into his memory. Singed into his brain with no chance of his forgetting. Not now he understood how little he'd meant to the man he'd spent years calling Dad. A loving term it turned out he'd had no right to use.

The sudden blast of a car horn interrupted Logan's heavy and grave thoughts. Strolling over to the French doors, he pushed back the sheer net curtains and turned the key in the lock. Stepping out on to the narrow balcony, he let the warm sunshine and the smells from the restaurant float to him once again, dispelling some of the bleakness of his mood.

Leaning over the lush trailing plants and the railing, he waved to the driver in the taxi below.

Time to return to England and finish with the past for good. To track down the one person who might know the truth concerning the whole deplorable situation surrounding his birth. The older sibling Logan hadn't seen for years. Maddox, his elusive half-brother.

'Those babies need a father.'

Thurza Bow rolled her eyes and lifted the four-pack of super-soft toilet rolls out of the cardboard box, fighting the urge to throw the item at her cousin's head. Sometimes the itch to be wicked took hold when she was in Rachel's company. A dreadful but unfortunate truth.

Just for once Thurza ached to throw respect, good manners and decency to one side and give her nagging cousin the shock of her life. Besides, the toilet rolls were soft—it said so on the purple wrapping. So they wouldn't hurt…much.

'What you really need is to call the twins' father to account and force him to do his part in parenting. Don't you think it's time Daddy took a turn?'

Thurza placed another pack of toilet paper on to the shelf. 'He's not interested.'

'He's their father. He gets no choice. It's not right how he gets to walk away and leave you with the consequences of your joint sexual pleasure.'

Thurza glanced at her cousin. 'It's my choice to keep him out of our lives.'

'You're lying,' Rachel replied bluntly. 'You may tell yourself that nonsense, but I know you're hiding something.'

Thurza frowned, wondering if her cousin had resumed learning witchcraft. Lately, she had an uncanny knack of being right over most things. It was most annoying. 'I'm not lying. The man is unsuitable father material.'

Rachel scoffed. 'Didn't stop you sleeping with him.'

'At the time I wasn't considering him as a prospective father. I just sought a night of uncomplicated sex.'

Rachel sighed and shook her head. 'More lies. You don't do one-night stands, so the reason the twins' father tempted you into breaking your normal code of behaviour must be more than you're admitting to.'

Thurza slammed the final toilet roll pack down on to the shelf and retrieved the empty cardboard box. She hated how her cousin knew her so well.

Making her way towards the rear storeroom, she asked, 'Do you have everything you need today?'

'As you don't sell cousins with sense, I guess so,' Rachel returned sarcastically.

Thurza threw the box into the back room, hoping Rachel would leave, so she could resume shelf-filling and daydreaming about the one man she wasn't supposed to dream about. The man they were unfortunately discussing. A man who was truly forbidden and lost to her. Who had turned out to be the worst kind of jerk after their long illicit night together.

Rachel took her time picking up her bag of shopping. 'At least think about joining one of those dating sites I sent you the links for the other day. I'm sure even with your picky taste you can find someone. You do still have that list I gave you of local men with potential, don't you?'

'Somewhere…' Thurza hedged, not about to admit that she'd deleted both the links and the list from her phone five minutes after her cousin had sent them.

'You're a good-looking woman with that Viking female warrior vibe you're rocking. God, why did I have to take after my mother?' Rachel complained. 'Who wants little Miss Mousy Hair?'

'At least your mother lives close by,' Thurza pointed out.

Her father had died ten years before and her Swedish mother had left England not long after, to go and live in France with a French film director she'd met on a singles' mountain-climbing holiday.

Rachel scoffed. 'At least yours comes with the bonus of a holiday in France whenever you fancy it. Anyway, think about what I said.'

Thurza sighed. 'The boys and I are fine as we are. I'm twenty-seven years old, Rachel. I can manage my life on my own, thanks.'

'Yeah, right… You managed to leave this town and what happened? You returned, having left a very good nursing job, four months pregnant with no willing man to help. Let's not even touch the subject of contraception, Nurse Bow. Something, dear cousin, you apparently forgot the second your knickers hit the floor.'

Warmth flooded Thurza's cheeks. 'It was an unexpected encounter and we used contraception. My mistake came from trusting it to work.'

Rachel snorted and headed for the exit. 'You're the type of person who will always be in that unlucky two per cent failure rate, I'm afraid.'

The words stung, but Thurza refused to react. She had already accepted her mistake in giving in to the man's charms, without her cousin rubbing it in because the contraception they'd used had failed.

Letting out a sigh of relief when Rachel

finally left the shop and jumped into a small white van with the local chemist's logo on the side, Thurza reluctantly considered her cousin's suggestion.

Should she encourage a man into her and the boys' lives? She closed her eyes and shook her head. No, she didn't want a man hanging around, getting in the way and disrupting her calm and normality. The encounter with the twins' father had been nothing but one foolish moment of yielding to basic physical needs and ignoring the sensible inner voice that had warned her of the risk. For one night she'd given in to the irrational urge to be *seen* by a sexy doctor. A special evening when she'd become as attractive and as sexy as all the other nurses who worked at the hospital, instead of the shy woman people hardly noticed.

That out-of-character night had resulted in her becoming a mother to two beautiful baby boys.

She didn't regret her sons. Right from the moment she'd found out she was expecting them something had clicked and finally made sense in her life, had given her a true purpose.

She'd tried to let the man know about the pregnancy. Sent letter after letter to his flat during it. Once she'd even turned up on his doorstep, eight months pregnant, to be told by his cleaner that he had gone away for a while and she wasn't sure when he would be back.

She'd even sent a card after the twins' first smiles, when an attack of sadness had hit her at all the man was missing. Just like her letters, it had gone unanswered.

Yes, Dr Logan Fox's interest had vanished almost as quickly as his attraction to her. One night of lovemaking and then all those pretty sweet words he'd whispered in her ear as he'd taken her to a place she'd never dreamt existed between a man and woman had disappeared quicker than a twig dropped into the centre of a scorching hot fire.

She'd not received one answer or acknowledgement from him. Not a phone call, a note—not a single thing except a telling silence.

She could have pursued the legal option, but she refused to force a man into having a relationship with his offspring when he'd made it clear he didn't want one. She just wished he'd told her to her face, so she could live without the occasional qualm or doubt.

Thurza reached for another large container full of toilet rolls. No, she didn't need the man or his reluctant help. The twins deserved better than an uninterested father. She'd quite like some spare hours in the day, and a new washing machine that didn't sound as though it was on the verge of taking off every time she used it. But both were impossible wishes, so Thurza did what every other single parent did and sucked it up with a smile.

Because her boys were her happiness and they fulfilled her life. She just wished her cousin would one day understand that.

Logan pulled into a space in the garage's parking area, relieved to finally be in Dorset and close to where his half-brother Maddox lived. Soon he would be able to get the answers he'd come here for. The answers that would finally settle everything from the past and allow him to move on from it for good.

Gripping the hire car's steering wheel, he sighed. After years of no contact, he had to talk to his estranged half-brother. The half-brother who'd walked out of the family home on his twenty-first birthday and never returned. The sibling Logan had always believed he could trust, despite their lack of communication over the years.

Logan wanted to stare into his face and hear the whole and complete story. Not hostile statements parroted through a dead man's solicitor's letter. A full explanation from someone Logan suspected knew everything. He wanted to see with his own eyes the moment when his half-brother realised that he knew of their mother's long-ago infidelity, and then watch him try and squirm out of answering Logan's questions. Because he had many.

His so-called family—the people who were supposed to support and care for him, to love him, even—had all lied to him. Individuals who'd regularly over the years lectured him on loyalty had shown him none. For them the trait had become unimportant and insignificant when compared to the hope of one day gaining favour and eventually a decent share of Victor's wealth. A selfish goal that not one of them had actually achieved.

In the Fox family a person accepted and played their role. For him it had required being the perfect son. The one who'd achieved more than the disappointing older sibling. He'd had to do what Victor expected, when it was required. And Logan had done just that for years, without resentment or complaint, because he had cared about the man.

But now he refused to be disregarded or ignored. In the next few hours his dear half-brother was going to spill the truth whether he wanted to or not. He owed Logan. Even if he had to wring it out of Maddox syllable by drawn-out syllable.

Reaching for his phone where it lay on the passenger's seat, next to an empty takeaway coffee cup, a half-eaten ham sandwich and an unused paper napkin, Logan flicked through the long list of contacts until he found his half-brother's name and punched the button.

He'd discovered Maddox's whereabouts after finding a postcard amongst the wad of papers the solicitor had handed him when he'd collected his belongings from the family house in Salisbury. Sent over a year ago, it had Maddox's address and phone number scribbled on it. Nothing else—no greeting or comment—just his name, address and mobile number.

The solicitor had found it while sorting through Victor's study. Hidden at the back of a drawer in the old man's desk, as though he hadn't been able to bring himself to throw it away, but hadn't wanted anyone else to see it either.

Drumming his fingertips against the leather steering wheel, Logan waited as unanswered rings purred in his ear.

After at least twenty rings, his half-brother's voice finally growled down the line. 'What?'

'How do I get to your place?' Logan demanded, too irritated to care about pleasantries or polite greetings. This close to getting his answers, he'd given up any pretence of patience or manners.

Removing his glasses, he rubbed the bridge of his nose, and pushed back the weariness that hovered close.

Tense silence answered his demand.

'I said, *brother*, how do I get to your home?' he repeated, biting out the words with icy firmness.

If Maddox imagined he could put him off, then he intended to prove differently. Wherever the man resided in this godforsaken seaside town, Logan would find him and force him to have a long overdue conversation.

'Logan?' Maddox barked. 'What the hell do you want?'

After years of no contact, Logan wasn't offended by his sibling's less than friendly greeting. 'I'm in Dorset, in the town where you live, and I'm not leaving until we talk.'

Silence returned, before a heavy sigh came from his half-brother. 'What's happened?'

'Victor's dead.'

'When?'

'Ten weeks ago.'

Logan forced away the flood of sentimental emotion saying the words pulled from his heart. The man had lied to him his whole life, and only when he knew he wouldn't face the consequences of that deception had he made certain that his fake son discovered the truth. When he'd no longer needed Logan to ease his old age loneliness Victor had cut him off. Thrown Logan and his love away like redundant, useless objects he no longer wished to possess. The man didn't deserve his grief or his tears, and he refused to give in to either.

'The old man told you, didn't he?' said Maddox.

Logan's fingers tightened around the phone. The small pathetic hope that his half-brother might not know the truth withered and died. His instinct had been sadly right once again.

'In a way. He left instructions with his solicitor to inform me of the truth regarding my parentage after his death.'

Further silence settled between them, before Maddox sighed again. 'I guess you'd better come to the farm.'

Logan grabbed the napkin from the passenger seat and pulled a pen from his shirt pocket. In silence, he wrote down the instructions Maddox gave him.

Finishing the call, Logan decided he might as well get some fuel while he was there, and drove round to the fuel pumps. He glanced out through the windscreen at his surroundings. A large plastic kangaroo tied to the garage's shop roof bobbed around in the breeze. The sight was an apt reflection of the sensations inside him.

Replacing his glasses, Logan opened the car door. The ache in his chest refused to ease and continued to grow and intensify. Damn emotions. Why couldn't they just stay stuffed down where he'd shoved them? He didn't have the time or the inclination to deal with them.

After his conversation with his half-brother, he intended never to think about Victor again. He planned to cut his last remaining ties with England and fly out before the end of the week. Whether he'd return to Malta or head somewhere new he didn't know.

His eyes shifted to the shop, his gaze drawn towards the large window and the woman who stood inside. A strange, unfamiliar tingling surfaced from the deep recesses of his stomach, slowly prickling and twisting through his whole body.

Staring harder at the woman, he took in her appearance, slowly moving his gaze over the mustard-yellow top she was wearing to rest on her long blonde hair and strong Nordic features. She looked familiar. Like someone he'd once briefly known—in the physical sense, anyway. A woman who'd tempted him to do unfamiliar and sinful things he'd never tried before. Someone whose sweet, gorgeous body he'd explored intimately during one long night.

Someone whose sweet, kissable and frankly too enticing mouth he still dreamt about all these months later.

Logan swallowed hard, unable to pull his gaze away. His heart kicked up its pace until it banged painfully against his chest. The woman didn't just resemble the woman from that night—he was pretty certain it really was her.

Turning away, he ran a palm over his face while his mind raced. Focusing on the petrol pump, he grabbed the nozzle and filled the car's tank. Wasting time as he tried to make sense of the situation.

Okay, play it cool, Fox. Go inside, pay and leave. Pretend you don't recognise her. If she tries to drag you into conversation or tries to get reacquainted, leave fast. You've more important things to do than revisiting an ex-lover, even if she did provide the best night of lovemaking you've ever known.

She was the only woman he'd ever shared a one-night stand with. The woman he'd taken to bed mere days after calling off his doomed engagement, only to wake up and find her gone the next morning, leaving him with nothing but the scent of her fading perfume on his love-wrinkled bed sheets and a heart full of regrets.

Was some higher figure messing with him as punishment for a crime he didn't recall? First Victor's death, his painful rejection, and now an awkward meetup with a past lover. Together with the upcoming meeting with his half-brother, these last few months were rounding off to be a blinder.

Sliding the pump back into its rest, Logan replaced the car's fuel cap and glanced again at the woman inside the building.

Bite the bullet, Fox, and face her.

With a deep breath, he wiped his damp palms against his trousers and took a step towards the building and his one lapse of sanity. The thudding of his heartbeat echoed loudly in his ears with each step closer to the woman he'd done his best to forget.

Not that he'd succeeded. For eighteen months this woman and their time together had repeatedly taunted him on those nights when the clock had ticked sluggishly through the dark night hours and he'd been alone in a huge bed with only his frustrated thoughts and memories to keep him company.

A goddess in bed, with skin soft and smooth,

and a sweet naughty mouth which had taught him some moves he'd never known before. Hair like a Viking queen's and an accent that had rocked between low Dorset tones and a faint sexy Swedish lilt.

That night he'd recognised her from the corridors in the hospital where they'd both worked. Her wonderful fresh eagerness for the job had yet to be dimmed by long, endless shifts and the never-ending conveyor belt of patients.

What he'd discovered once he'd taken her home was that beneath her clothes was a body made to entrance and seduce a man. In that ultimate, exquisite moment when their bodies had joined, he knew he'd experienced heaven for the first time.

Or maybe he'd just imagined it. Envisaged the memory of her sweet soft moans and angelic gasps to make his dented confidence feel better. So that despite all the turmoil in his life at that time, the woman in his bed had really wanted him as much as he'd wanted her.

His gaze returned to the window, his unease increasing when he noted her expression. Was that horror on her face? Really?

Unexpected disappointment rushed through him at the same time as a loud, high-pitched scream sounded across the forecourt, freezing him to the spot.

Twisting in the direction of the scream, he spotted another vehicle with two squabbling young boys and a woman standing next to it. After a moment, the woman picked up one child and put him into the rear seat of the car.

'Let me see,' she instructed the remaining boy, who stood clutching his right eye while screaming at the top of his voice. 'What did Troy stab you with?'

'His toy screwdriver!'

With all thoughts of the woman inside the building and her lack of welcome on pause, Logan walked purposefully towards the injured boy. Facing the complications of his past could wait. Right now a child needed his medical expertise, and that took priority over everything.

CHAPTER TWO

THURZA GULPED AS her one past mistake walked away from the building and headed in the direction of the mother and child beside the second car on the forecourt. Gripping the blue cloth she was using to wipe a dirty smudge from the windowpane, she briefly tussled between whether to run out through the back door and away from the complications the man's unexpected arrival represented, or head outside and help the six-foot-two bulge of hard muscle and inflated ego she'd once stupidly shared an unforgettable night with.

Glancing at her shaking hands, she drew in a deep breath and went to grab the first aid kit. She was a nurse. She would do whatever was needed to help the child and ignore the man now striding across the forecourt.

But what if Logan Fox recognised her? Not an impossibility. Not really. Considering they'd once shared a night together. After all, he'd explored and tasted intimate areas of her body no other man ever had. But she'd prefer he didn't. Then she could return to forgetting him—which wasn't easy considering she lived with two small reminders who were his image, and also her constant and unfortunate habit of daydreaming about him.

But imagine having to explain to her sons in future years that, yes, she had seen their father again, but sadly, he hadn't recognised her, and had instead stared blankly into her face as though she were a stranger. Crushing—not only for her own self-confidence—and hardly the candy heart stuff of happy families that children hoped to hear where their parents were concerned.

She pushed the door open and a cold breeze greeted her, causing a full-body shiver to join her internal shaking. Great. By the time she joined the group she'd probably be a mass of quivers inside and out.

Swallowing the dryness from her mouth, and with slow, reluctant steps, she walked towards the trio. Mass fluttering swelled inside her stomach as she approached, her eyes skimming hesitantly over the man's white shirt and dark trousers, before working their way back up the line of his spine to linger for a traitorous second or two on his wide shoulders.

Fighting her natural nursing instinct, which was clamouring to push in and take over treating the still yelling child, Thurza stopped a few paces away from the group. 'Er...excuse me? Can I help?'

She waited for a reply, but all she obtained was a distracted glance from the boy's mother, before the woman returned her attention to the man now softly talking to the boy.

After a moment, Thurza gave in to the inevitable and crouched beside Logan, accidentally bumping his arm as she bent. *Oh, fiddles.* It felt as firm as she remembered. All hard muscle and solid tissue. Pulling back from the unexpected contact, she swallowed hard and tried to ignore the sizzling impression it had left on her own body. Inappropriate reactions and thoughts were not wanted right now.

'It's okay,' she said gently to the boy, forcing herself to concentrate on the injured child and not the brief moment of physical connection she'd just experienced. 'We're here to help you feel better. What's your name?'

'Fr-Fr-Freddie,' the boy stuttered out in between wails.

'Hello, Freddie. I've brought our first aid kit

so we can help you,' said Thurza. Logan continued trying to soothe the hysterical child, not glancing her way. 'What happened?' she asked Logan, also keeping her eyes firmly focused on Freddie.

'Thank you for bringing the kit. This young man has sustained an injury to his eye, and it needs to be stabilised until he can get to a hospital for further investigation.'

'Will he be all right?' demanded the mother, who was on Logan's other side. 'One moment they were laughing and singing, the next he was screaming his head off.'

'Let's concentrate on saving your son's eyesight, shall we?' Logan replied gently. 'Questions can wait for the moment.'

The mother nodded and moved a little closer to her son. Thurza noted the movement had also brought her closer to Logan.

'Why don't you tell me what happened, Freddie?' Logan asked, his voice quiet but firm now he'd coaxed the child down from his hysterical wailing.

Sobbing, Freddie said, 'Troy stabbed me with his toy screwdriver.'

Logan winced. 'Ouch, I bet that hurt.'

'It's agony,' the boy answered dramatically. 'I hate him.'

'Did it go right into your eye or just catch

your eyelid?' Logan quizzed, ignoring the last part of Freddie's remark.

Thurza hid a smile, though. It was a universal truth that all siblings hated one another at some point during their childhood years. She doubted this would be the last time the boy thought or uttered those or similar words.

'Right in. It won't stop watering and it hurts bad.'

Thurza opened the box and took out a pair of sterile gloves, offering them to Logan. 'Here. We should have everything you need. I keep it well stocked.'

Logan finally turned to Thurza and met her gaze. The strong flash of recognition shone in his dark blue eyes as they silently searched her face, triggering another quiver to surge through her. Every part of her body, inside and out, throbbed from the power of that look.

'Thank you,' he said.

Breath wedged in her throat like a large roughly peeled raw potato. Thurza found herself unable to look away. The face that had plagued her for months and months had now physically materialised in front of her. All sane thought vanished as she took in the strong jaw, dark cheeks and long, straight nose. When his eyes dropped lower, to rest on her mouth, she noticed his curly lashes and the perfect arch of his eyebrows, gorgeously magnified by his glasses.

No dictionary in the world could possibly hold an adjective to truly describe the male beauty in front of her. The man was physically stunning.

Forcing herself to remember the way he'd used her for one night and ignored her later attempts at contact, she dragged her gaze away and fixed her attention on the contents of the first aid box. Time to stop dithering and do her job. The one she was trained to do.

Falling back on her nursing professionalism, she waited silently as Logan once again spoke to the child.

'Right, Freddie. Please keep your head absolutely still for me while I take a quick look at your eye. Can you do that?'

Seeing the calm, patient way he dealt with the young boy pulled at her heart. Were there other Fox children running around? Were hers the only ones he'd chosen to ignore? The notion caused another squeeze to her heart, and a new wave of dislike for the male at her side washed over Thurza.

The child nodded, until Thurza reached out and stopped him. With an encouraging smile, she suggested, 'How about we ask your mum to come and stand behind you, so she can hold your head while the doctor has a look?'

She motioned to the mother, who shifted behind her son and did as Thurza directed, gently cupping the sides of Freddie's head with her palms.

'I'm going to move your hand,' Logan encouraged Freddie. 'I won't hurt you. I just need to take a quick look.'

Freddie stood quietly as Logan gently lowered the hand covering the boy's eye and silently studied the child's streaming eyeball before he spoke to Thurza. 'I can't see any visible damage, but it is extremely bloodshot. I think it's best to be cautious and pop to a hospital…get the doctors there to take a proper look.'

'Is it really that bad?' the mother asked.

'Without the proper equipment I can't answer that,' Logan replied honestly. 'To be sure, you'll need someone at a hospital to check him over. They have the right equipment to do a thorough examination of the eyeball.'

The woman sighed and lowered her hands from her son's head. 'I knew we should never have bought that children's tool set. I told my husband it was a bad idea. The boys are always fighting and doing stupid things like this to each other.'

'Would you mind handing me a sterile pad and a roll of bandaging?' Logan asked Thurza.

Thurza collected a clean pad and a fresh dressing from the first aid box.

Logan took the pad and positioned it gently against Freddie's eye. 'I need you to keep both your eyes still, Freddie. No looking from side to side or rolling them up and down. Just perfectly still. Not only now, but right up until you see a doctor at the hospital. I know it's hard, but if you don't it could cause further damage to your eye.'

With a nod Thurza's way, Logan held the pad, while she efficiently and quickly wrapped the bandage round the child's head to hold the protective wadding in place. Her unsteady fingers brushed Logan's as she made a final loop around Freddie's head. The touch tingled through her, but she shook it away and focused on her task. The sooner it was completed, the quicker they could all pile back into their vehicles and leave.

Happy that both the bandage and pad were secure, she tied off the dressing and returned the remaining bandage to the box. Once again, she glanced at the good-looking man at her side. Why did God make some men handsome, but also complete and utter jack-asses, too? Was it some devious test to see how many women weakened and succumbed to the effects of a roguish smile? Well, she'd failed dismally, having surrendered to this man's smile and more.

To think she'd once kissed those cheeks during their brief romp together. Kissed most of his body. And licked it. Goodness, how she had licked and explored inches of his smooth skin.

Concentrate, Bow. You're a trained nurse and this is a medical emergency. Nothing to do with a man or an ex-lover. He means noth-ing to you, and you definitely do not still find any part of Dr Logan Fox attractive. Stop the naughty thoughts right this second.

Picking up the box, she straightened at the same time as Logan. Why was he in town? Had he finally grown a conscience after months of silence and decided that he needed to see her and the boys? Or, worse, had he suddenly concluded that he wanted to be in their lives?

Dr Logan Fox in her life permanently? A different kind of shudder leapt through her body, chilling her bones to the very marrow.

Oh, no, that was not a good idea. Not after he'd kept his distance for so long.

She pushed away the disturbing thought and pulled her mobile from her trouser pocket. She waved it and asked Freddie's mother, 'Shall I phone for an ambulance?'

Logan also focused on the mother, both his gaze and his silence expectant.

'No, I'll take him,' the woman replied, placing a reassuring arm around her son's shoulders. 'It will probably be quicker than waiting for one to arrive. Plus, I have my other kids in the car.'

Logan nodded. 'Good sight is a precious gift. I would hate your child to lose any of his through a silly squabble with his brother.'

'Thank you for your help,' Freddie's mother said. 'Both of you. Thank you.'

In silence, Thurza and Logan watched the mother help Freddie into the back seat of the car and then drive off in the direction of the closest hospital.

'Do you think he'll be okay?' Thurza asked, not knowing what else to say now they were alone. He'd made no verbal indication to confirm that he definitely recognised her, but a tautness hummed between them. As though their bodies had silently identified one another, despite their efforts to pretend differently.

'I think so. No doubt the child who caused the injury and the father who bought the tool set will suffer an earful later.'

Thurza nodded, hesitantly pointing to the building behind them. 'Well, I need to fill out an incident report.'

Logan rolled off the gloves and dumped them in a nearby bin. 'I need to pay for my fuel.'

'Oh, you can do that at the pump with your card,' Thurza said in a moment of panic, and then she lied. 'The tills are down inside. Sorry.'

Her heart racing, she scurried back towards the building, hoping Logan would do as she suggested. She wanted the man gone. Away from the garage, away from Dorset and, more importantly, far away from her baby sons.

Thurza let out a heavy sigh and waved goodbye to her boss. Wrapping her cream hand-knitted scarf around her neck, she shoved her hands into her coat pockets and headed for home. Turning in the direction of the cottage she rented, she hurried along the poorly lit country road.

Hopefully, she would have a chance to

warm the house through before her cousin arrived with the twins. As much as Rachel drove her mad, Thurza wouldn't be able to manage without her help in collecting the boys from day care twice a week and her frequent offers to babysit.

When Thurza had returned home pregnant, Rachel's disappointment had been her main concern. But her cousin had taken one look at Thurza's obvious baby bump, rolled her eyes the way she always did when she concluded that Thurza was beyond help then dragged her into a big hug which had left them both crying on the doorstep.

Thurza had needed that hug more than anything. Sometimes she still did.

Thurza smiled, feeling a whoosh of love for her cousin and her sons. The boys hadn't been planned, but she loved them with every part of her being. From the moment she'd discovered they were growing inside her, she'd sworn to give her children the best home possible and oodles of love.

Which brought her back to the question that had been constantly revolving through her mind since the earlier incident at the garage. Prodding at her consciousness until it left her with a thumping headache. Why was Dr Logan Fox in town? What had brought him to this part of Dorset? Was he just visiting, passing through, or did he have another motive for his unexpected arrival? One that involved her and the boys? One she unquestionably wasn't going to like?

Though he hadn't said anything to confirm that he remembered her, she'd seen it in his gaze when he'd turned and spoken to her. Those blue eyes had given their own confirmation. Speech was unnecessary when their bodies instinctively did the communicating for them.

On the other hand, he'd also got back in his car and left after paying for his fuel. So maybe his arrival in town was nothing to worry over. Just an unplanned momentary glitch in both their lives. One best forgotten.

Not for a second did Thurza see Logan Fox as a fan of Dorset's autumnal countryside. White Caribbean sands and fruity cocktails handed out by accommodating staff were more his style. Definitely more Monaco or the Bahamas than Dorset beaches and earthy leaf-covered forests. No wet Sunday afternoon walks or muddy boots for him.

Yet here he was, in a town which took less than ten minutes to drive through and over twenty-five minutes to find on a map. They had a beautiful coast and an award-winning farm shop and tea rooms, but agriculture remained the main economy in the area, not tourism.

The question remained unanswered. Why had Logan Fox arrived in Dorset? Had he left now or was he still hanging around somewhere while he figured out his next move? Did his presence indicate a wish to make contact after all the letters Thurza had sent to him? Letters she'd initially poured her heart into, until it had become clear he wasn't interested in her or her progressing pregnancy. If so, why hadn't he mentioned them while at the garage? Why hadn't he enquired after the boys? Was he waiting for the right moment to offer her money and forget his connection to their sons, or perhaps he intended to find out more about her life first?

But why would he want to do that?

She frowned and dug her hands deeper into her coat pockets. Was he in town because he hoped to discover some terrible local scandal which involved her, so that he could steal her babies and then try to cut her out of their lives?

She stumbled on a broken piece of Tarmac, barely noticing the pain shooting through her toes as that last thought vibrated through her heart. She gasped as the idea grew, feeling her body tense as her imagination flew. Was that it? Did he hope to take her children away? Was he plotting right this minute to use his wealth and reputation to remove them from her care?

Closing her eyes, she sucked in a deep breath of cold night air and shook her head. Coerced her sickening thoughts back into calm, rational ones. Her unruly imaginings were a strong overreaction, thanks to the man's appearance in town. It was probably nothing more than a horrible coincidence. One best disregarded. Rather like their long-ago night together. No point in hysterics when there was probably no reason for them.

But the small niggle of doubt refused to be hushed completely. The man had definitely recognised her. No matter how much she wished differently. That clear flicker of awareness had shone too brightly between them to ignore or deny. So why hadn't he said something?

Her mind bouncing up and down like a set of old-fashioned out-of-control scales, she scolded herself for pondering over Logan Fox at all. The man didn't deserve her time, or the effort of her agitated thoughts. She'd done her best to let him know about the boys. How much more was she supposed to do? It was he who had snubbed her efforts and refused to include himself in their children's lives, not the other way around.

After all, they were practically strangers, despite the fact she'd given birth to his children. But nobody in town knew that, and she intended to make certain it stayed her secret.

Thurza turned into the narrow lane that led to her home. Originally they had been staff cottages, attached to the large country estate where a B-movie actress from the 1970s now resided. The local council had purchased them over twenty years ago and now rented them out to locals.

She'd suffered through hours of labour without Logan Fox's help. He'd not rubbed her aching back on those nights when sleep had refused to come because unborn twins took up a lot of room inside a woman's body. No, he'd done nothing to help her. To him she was just a woman he'd slept with. Interesting and attractive for a few hours, but no more.

And what was he to her? Well, he'd been nothing but a convenient sexual partner for a single night. Pretty mediocre sex, too. At least that was what she told herself on the nights when she woke up feeling hot and achy from dreaming about him. Hating herself for twisting and turning beneath her duvet for a man who hadn't cared once he'd had his enjoyment.

Logan Fox had ignored her letters informing him about his impending fatherhood and carried on with his life. And today he driven away, making it obvious that he regarded her and their sons as insignificant. And for that, more than anything, she truly hated him.

With a heavy sigh she pulled her house keys from her pocket and let herself into the dark cottage. If Logan Fox did choose to bring a fight to her door, then he'd find her no easy pushover. She loved her children too much to ever be fooled by him and his charm again.

Lips, kissable and willing. Lips he ached to slowly nibble and suck. To learn their divine taste and enjoy their softness. Lips he prayed to feel pressing light, feather-soft caresses all over his hot, sensitive skin. Starting at the curve of his shoulder before slowly, eagerly, gliding across his chest and lower, to the spot where her kisses felt so very good...

The sound of ridiculously loud music dragged Logan from the wonderful sensations and ruined his concentration on what he hoped the woman in his dream would do next. He desperately grasped for the ebbing

sweetness, anxious to return to that delightful unconscious state where wondrous warm
pleasure lifted his mood and put his world
upright.

The music grew louder.

What the heck was going on?

Reluctantly, Logan opened his eyes and
slowly focused on the unfamiliar surroundings. An ugly brass-and-wood ceiling light
filled his vision, and there was the smell of
fried chips cooked in lard. *Gross.*

'What the hell…?' he groaned, rubbing a
hand across his forehead as thankfully the
music was turned off. He took in the large
black flat-screen television, a wooden coffee table scattered with sports magazines, an
array of used coffee mugs and numerous re-
mote controls. Wherever this messy hell was,
it certainly wasn't his home. Being close to
this much disorder made his skin itch.

He moaned once more and tried to sit up,
to get his bearings and clear his head.

'Finally!' a familiar voice boomed from
somewhere behind him.

The past twenty-four hours came back
and hit Logan with the force of a tumbling
log. The flight back to England, the solicitor
in Salisbury, the drive to Dorset and finally
Maddox. There was something else, too, there

on his mental horizon, just out of reach but tantalising all the same. Something important but disinclined to come forward. If only he could remember what or who it was…

Shifting on the sofa, Logan sat up. Rubbing his eyes, he used the time to get his thoughts straight before he started demanding answers from his sibling.

He groaned as the image of a pair of female lips flittered through his mind. God, could he not link several words into a sentence without her sweet mouth penetrating his thoughts?

The thing he struggled to recall hovered once again on the edges of his memory, but still refused to materialise. He could swear it was major and significant. Definitely something crucial.

Maddox appeared in front of him. Six foot and with all the packed muscles of an ex-soldier turned farmer. He wore a faded grey T-shirt and a dirty pair of khaki trousers. Other than a few extra wrinkles and grey strands running through his dark curls, his much older half-brother looked to be the same arrogant bonehead he remembered.

'I suppose you're here to tell me the old man left you everything?' he said.

Logan almost laughed. If only it were that simple.

'No, I'm here because I want answers, and as Mum's no longer around to give them, you're the only one I can ask. Is it true? Am I really the result of an affair she had with one of Victor's business partners?'

Maddox froze. 'What? I thought he just told you about the affair...not the rest.'

Logan cringed at his choice of words. 'The rest'? Was that a summary of his existence? Was he nothing but the human evidence of others' past actions and happenings, without real meaning or significance?

After several seconds, Maddox asked, 'Did you never wonder why you don't resemble Victor? You don't look much like Mum or me either. Yeah, we both inherited her dark colouring, but I take after my Italian father, whereas you could walk into any Bollywood film set and be offered the male starring role.'

Maddox had a point, but Logan had always figured his colouring stemmed from some long-forgotten relative no one recollected, but whose genes showed up every few generations.

'How long have you known?'

Maddox dropped on to a nearby armchair. 'From the moment I found her crying on the day she discovered she'd conceived you.'

Logan swallowed hard, his heart twingeing at the words. Crying didn't sound good. Crying indicated disappointment and unhappiness. Regret. 'Didn't she want me?'

'Of course she did,' Maddox snapped. 'You and your father—the real one—but she knew if she tried to leave Victor he'd have enjoyed destroying her and your dad's lives. She worried that he'd turn his anger on us as well. You know what a petty mean-minded man Victor became when he was crossed. She was too scared to risk ruining our lives. But she loved your father. Even as a spotty teenager I understood that.'

'Why didn't you tell me?' Logan asked. Out of everyone, he'd always believed Maddox could be trusted. Yet, it appeared his half-brother had taken part in the charade and the lies as much as the rest of the family.

'Not for me to say. And when you were born Victor acted smitten with you. Carried you everywhere. Showed you off like one of those fancy business awards he won. I figured he didn't know the truth and thought it best to leave that particular family skeleton alone. If Mum had wanted you to know she would have told you when she became ill. I think in the end she found it easier to continue the fantasy she'd formed over the years to keep everyone she loved safe.'

Logan rose from the sofa, wobbling slightly as he tried to keep both his balance and his temper. He understood Maddox's desire to protect their mother—they'd always been close—but what about him? Didn't his feelings count?

'You all lied to me, Maddox. I had a right to know the truth.'

'And Mum had a right to her secrets. Look, if I'd realised Victor was biding his time, waiting to get even, then I'd have told you,' Maddox said. 'But I honestly thought he cared about you.'

Logan snorted. Yeah, he'd stupidly thought Victor cared, too. The pathetic truth was that nobody really had. They might have told themselves they were protecting him, but hadn't it been more the case that they'd wanted to protect themselves and hide their past indiscretions?

Logan believed his half-brother. He didn't want to, but the sincerity in Maddox's voice and eyes convinced him. He didn't forgive him, but he did believe him. It still hurt, though. To think that all the people he'd grown up around and put faith in had continually lied. That there wasn't one family member he could stare in the face and know he could trust their word.

If he ever fathered a child Logan would never lie to it. He'd be in its life no matter what. But after the mistakes he'd made in the past—nearly marrying a woman he didn't love, walking away from another for reasons he'd never fully understood—he doubted it would happen. Love and relationships were not his forte. He didn't believe in the former and had created a pig's ear of the latter.

'It's good to see you anyway,' Logan said, realising he meant it. They might not be close now, but Maddox was still his half-brother and he'd missed him. 'We should keep in touch better.'

'Yeah, we should.' Maddox nodded.

Again, there was that hazy lurking sensation that refused to come to mind, that tiptoed out of reach. Like a whispered secret spoken just beyond his hearing. Compelling and thrilling, but frustratingly unknown. No matter how he tried to coax it, it refused his repeated beckoning.

'I'm sorry about Victor,' Maddox said. 'Nothing but a twisted son of a she-devil. But I know you loved him. Shame the man didn't appreciate the fact.'

Logan nodded, wanting to shut out everything. If he closed his eyes and breathed deeply perhaps it would all disappear for a while.

A too-familiar set of lips drifted into his subconscious once again, but with practised ease he mentally pushed them away and...

That was it!

He straightened, the memory that had refused to materialise finally coming to him. It was her. The woman who had haunted his dreams for over a year. She was here. Not in Maddox's house, but working at the local garage. She'd helped him treat the boy with the eye injury.

Rubbing a hand over his chest, he felt the unwelcome attraction he'd hoped he'd finally buried while living in Malta stir and re-emerge with fresh potency. All the feelings he'd struggled for months to submerge and deny flared with renewed enthusiasm and vigour.

Closing his eyes, Logan purposely slammed a figurative door between him and the reactions the woman evoked. He'd stay for a couple of weeks to reconnect with Maddox, and then leave for somewhere new. Somewhere no one knew him and he could start over. A warm location, far away from the woman and her persistent memory.

What he and Thurza Bow had once shared

was best left alone. Their lives had been linked for a short time, before parting again. One day, with luck and willpower, he'd finally stop thinking about her. Maybe find some other woman to fill his head.

God knew he yearned for the day when he could close his eyes without that woman drifting into his dreams…

CHAPTER THREE

THURZA WAVED GOODBYE to Mr Blakeman's daughter and left the large Edwardian house where she'd finished visiting one of the surgery's terminally ill patients. The illness that was taking over Alfred Blakeman's body might curtail some of his day-to-day abilities and enjoyment, but Thurza hoped that, together with the aid of her colleagues at the local doctor's surgery, who shared his care, she could make the man's twilight days as pain-free as possible.

Passing a row of traditional cottages that led to the seafront, Thurza felt her stomach growl longingly for the two slices of toast she planned to devour once she reached the surgery. Since starting that morning she had carried out five home visits, and was ready for a reviving late breakfast and a cup of tea before her shift ended at midday.

Thankfully all her visits that morning had

been within walking distance of the doctor's surgery. On the days she needed to travel outside of town she borrowed Rachel's car. It was cheaper for them to car-share—especially as her cousin had use of her firm's work van during the day.

Heading towards the beach promenade, rather than walking through the town, Thurza quickened her footsteps. With luck, she would catch the local lifeboat crew going through one of their weekly training sessions.

The sight of the boat skimming and crashing over the waves, especially at this time of year, aroused bittersweet memories in Thurza. Happy days from her childhood, when she would rush down to the beach before school and sit on the pebbles to watch. Smiling and waving when she spotted her father amongst the crew members.

On grey mornings like today she missed those happy days. Missed seeing her father's smile. Longed for the comfort and warmth it had always surrounded her with. She still craved one last chance to talk to him about everything and nothing, content simply to be in his company.

But on a similar morning, when the silver-toned grim sea had blended with the dark, overcast sky, her father had gone out with the crew on a rescue and never returned. A large wave had caught the vessel they'd rushed to help and turned it over, snatching her father into the watery depths at the same time. They'd recovered his lifeless body further along the coast several hours later. A freak accident, the coroner had called it. One that would probably never occur again.

Closing her eyes, Thurza held back the tears that still came, despite the loss being over ten years ago. She'd loved her father. Still loved him. He'd been her world and each day she grieved for him. An all too familiar emptiness sat inside her heart for all the memories they shared and for those that fate had robbed them from making. Although the pain of her father's death had faded over the years, the loneliness left behind hadn't.

What would he think of her now, as an adult? Working two jobs to keep herself and her two babies? If there really was a heaven, and he was watching from above, would he be proud of the person she'd grown into? Or disappointed by some of her choices? Would he love her sons as much as she did and see them as a precious gift? Or would he feel, as her mother did, that babies should come with a marriage certificate and old-fashioned respectability?

Would her father be disappointed with her for not only failing to keep the promise she'd once made him, but also for allowing fear to dictate that decision? Or would he understand that sometimes decisions in life weren't always clear-cut and simple? That emotions and experiences often ruled a person's choices, and that sometimes those other considerations took precedence over previously made vows?

With a heavy sigh, Thurza turned, pushing the sad memories and the heart-aching questions away. Tormenting herself over what her father would think was a waste of time. Her choices were hers to live with. Hers to justify to no one but herself. She just hoped that one day it would get easier, living with the knowledge that she had let him down.

Logan rolled over for the umpteenth time on the too-small sofa, slamming a cushion against his right ear in the hope of blocking out the sound of his older sibling's loud and irritating snoring.

Turning on to his back, he gave up on sleep and gripped the cushion against his chest. His eyes fixed on the early-morning shadows playing across the ceiling, and his thoughts returned to the previous day's events.

Being around Maddox after all this time had felt strange and oddly comforting.

Logan had come to Dorset for answers and now he finally had them. Enough to satisfy his curiosity anyway.

His mother had foolishly indulged in a doomed love affair with a man she could never have been with. Had she ever thought about her lover after she'd let him go? The man she'd saved from her husband's wrath and retribution? Had she really pushed him and their affair from her mind? Or had the sight of her child through the subsequent years traumatised her with memories of the ex-lover she could never be with and Logan would never know?

And the man? Did he ever consider the child he'd walked away from? Or was Logan's existence just a long-ago mistake in the man's life? One he no longer considered or recalled?

He sighed and stared at the ugly multicoloured material on the back of the sofa. After the initial shock of hearing that his mother had committed adultery, he'd tried hard not to dissect the information too deeply. He might know the facts and easily envisage the reasons why she'd sought physical comfort from another man, but he didn't want to examine it further. Was his mother's love life any of his business anyway?

And the man whom his mother had tried to protect? Did Logan want to know about the male who'd sired him and then walked away? Who had allowed a woman to stay in an unhappy marriage to save his own skin?

No, he carried no desire to find out more about the mysterious figure who had made the decision to stay out of Logan's life. A man not strong enough to fight for the woman who loved him or to put her happiness above everything else, even his own security.

Logan forced his fingers to loosen on the cushion and closed his eyes. He could only guess at what his mother had felt for the man she'd given up and her reasons for doing so.

Perhaps Maddox was wrong, and their mother had viewed the affair as nothing but a sexual folly with someone different and affectionate. Living with Victor might have included wealth and luxuries, but emotionally he'd starved the people around him. Except for Logan. Out of everyone in the family, Victor had shown him more warmth and affection than anyone.

That was why his rejection hurt so much. Despite Victor's many faults, Logan had truly believed he'd held affection for him.

Victor had raised him as his son. Attended every school play, parents' evening and sports event. When Logan had experienced a phase of bullying at the expensive private school he'd attended Victor had patiently listened to his complaints and then given advice on how to deal with the culprits over teacakes and glasses of lemonade. He'd encouraged and believed in Logan. Had always been there for him, far more than his mother ever had.

Then with his death everything had changed.

Instead of taking the unpleasant truth to the grave with him, Victor had chosen to destroy and ruin everything he and Logan had shared throughout the years. His decision to have his solicitor inform Logan of the truth had been not only cruel, but cowardly.

And that was what hurt the most. Not content for Logan only to find out the truth, he'd deprived him of the chance to confront him, making it clear how little he'd really meant to him.

Standing, Logan slipped on his shoes and grabbed his suit jacket from the end of the sofa, where he'd left it the previous night. Nabbing a stale iced bun from the breakfast bar, he bit into it with an appreciative moan. He needed to clear his head and stretch his legs before he faced another day around Maddox.

A crisp morning frost sent a shiver over Logan's skin as he stepped out of the warm house and closed the door. Buttoning his jacket, he made his way down the gravel path towards the large wooden gate leading on to the country lane. Maddox had mentioned that the short lane led straight to the seafront. Apparently, the town wasn't big, but it was friendly and had everything a person required.

Shoving the last piece of bun into his mouth, Logan put his hands into his trouser pockets and quickened his pace. A few days ago he'd walked in the Maltese sunshine—now he strolled along a damp leaf-covered lane, dodging shiny brown conkers and their spiky green shells, wishing he'd grabbed a jumper from his car to keep out the autumn chill.

He didn't care how friendly the local residents were, or not. He was only going to be in the area for a few weeks. Enough time to catch up with his brother, but not long enough to form friendships. If he took on some local locum work it would give him a chance to sort out the sale of his flat and then find another position abroad. England no longer held any reason for him to stay. He'd occasionally missed it while living in Malta, but now nothing but disappointment tainted the place for him. The country was no longer important now there was no one left in his life who required his consideration or attendance.

An image floated into his thoughts, but as usual he pushed it away. The woman from the garage meant nothing to him. An error in his past—hardly worth one thought, let alone the many his brain insisted on wasting on her. Unexpectedly seeing her again had just brought it all back. Nothing more. Looking into her beautiful eyes had simply reminded him of what they'd once shared.

He'd heard via a friend that she'd left the hospital they'd both worked at a few months after their night together. Perhaps she'd met someone after their fleeting interlude. Someone important to her. Someone who wasn't him.

He breathed in a lungful of crisp air, not sure why the idea of her moving on bothered him. Too late now for doubts and recriminations. Better to go forward than ponder over missed opportunities like a soppy fool. Better to put all his energy into forgetting her for good. Exactly the way he was determined to.

He didn't care any more that she'd left his flat the following morning without a word of goodbye. Nope, he wasn't interested in her reasons for sneaking away. Evidently she'd just wanted a night of lovemaking and nothing more.

Only...

Only something about Thurza Bow had told him that wasn't her way. The awkward way she'd first acted when they'd reached his bedroom that night... Her flushed cheeks as he'd peeled off her clothes and watched the colour in her face deepen when she did the same to him... It had caused him to wonder if she'd ever spent a night with someone before.

Kicking a conker in frustration, he crushed the uninvited speculations. What they'd shared no longer mattered. Two weeks and then he'd leave. Fourteen days of visiting his brother, and then he'd get started on the future. One that did not involve a green-eyed temptress or a phoney family of liars.

Coming to the seafront, he crossed the road that ran along the promenade—and immediately came face to face with the one woman he'd just bitterly sworn to avoid.

'You!'

Thurza stared at Logan, silently cursing her bad luck. Twice in two days was suspicious and in no way a fluke. Was he spying on her? Tracking her around town? Stalking her?

'Excuse me.'

She tried to move past Logan, figuring it better not to acknowledge the man any further, but he stepped the same way and prevented her.

'I know who you are. We were too busy yesterday to talk, and I'd made arrangements to see my brother, but I do remember you,' he declared, taking another step towards her. His gaze held a mixture of purpose with a faint trace of annoyance.

Thurza instinctively backed away, not in the mood for dealing with an ex-lover who plainly didn't appreciate seeing her again. She raised her hand to stop him coming closer, forgetting how their fleeting touch yesterday had left her restless for hours afterwards.

'I don't know who you think I am, but—' She broke off, suddenly distracted by the way he was watching her. How had she forgotten the unusual blue shade of his eyes? Or the serious intensity of his gaze? Perhaps she'd simply refused to remember, finding it easier to forget.

Yesterday a hurt child's needs had occupied him, but now he was focusing his full attention on her, for longer than a few moments.

'I know who you are,' he repeated, his tone grave, as though she was to blame for this unexpected meeting and he resented her appearance.

'Really?' she quizzed, not believing him. The likelihood of him actually recalling her name after all this time seemed pretty slim. Deciding to test her theory, she asked, 'What's my name, then?'

'Thurza Bow,' he said without a pause.

Pants, she cursed silently, narrowing her eyes. She honestly hadn't thought he'd remember.

Opting for indifference, she shook her head. 'Excuse me, but I have to go.'

He ignored her and said, 'We both worked at St Maria's hospital, though I left just after we met. And your name is like your mouth. Sweet and bow-shaped.'

Her resolve dwindled at the unexpectedly romantic and sweet words. Then reality and common sense returned, and a harsh reminder that for eighteen months this man had callously ignored her and their sons. Logan Fox might spout charming words and phrases, but that was as far as it went. He used women for sex, and when there were consequences— two, in her case—he ignored all attempts at contact.

'I've no idea what you're talking about,' she said, determined to continue with her act of ignorance. Because what other option was there now she'd started? 'Are you ill? Lost? Confused?'

His gorgeous eyes narrowed and his mouth tightened, causing small lines to appear on each side. 'No, I'm not. You are Thurza Bow and we once spent a night together, making frantic, exciting love.'

'Shh!' she hissed, glancing around to see if anyone had heard. The man who ran the small cafe situated on the beachfront looked their way, but more with casual curiosity than outright shock. 'Keep your voice down,' she said. 'I don't think the people out in the bay heard you.'

'Then stop pretending you don't recognise me,' he warned. 'Perhaps I should ask that man outside the cafe if he knows your name?'

He moved to go past her, but Thurza grabbed his arm to stop him, aware that if he did the fragile fabrication of her denial would disintegrate and collapse.

'You're crazy,' she told him.

'And you're lying,' he accused. 'Though I'm not sure why. Especially as our night together was fun.'

'Fun!' she squealed. *'Fun?'*

Their night together had been many things, but 'fun' wasn't one of them. Erotic, exciting and passionate. Hot and satisfying. But not fun. Fun indicated something frivolous and unimportant. A brief moment of pleasure, but nothing more.

Deciding to end the conversation before he irritated her further, Thurza glared at him. 'I need to get to work.'

'I only want to talk to you,' Logan said.

Which was exactly the last thing she cared to do. Months ago, perhaps—but not now. Too much disappointment and ill feeling had developed inside her heart for Thurza to give him an easy time. Did he really expect her to smile and be friendly? To welcome him like a long-lost friend she was pleased to see again after the cold way he'd turned his back on her and the boys? Well, no, she wasn't happy to see him, and she would rather not spend time with him. Not even for five minutes.

Digging up some of her long pent-up resentment, she snapped, 'Well, I'm afraid I don't want to speak to *you*. Especially considering you displayed no eagerness or desire to talk to me yesterday at the garage. In fact, I'm pretty sure you drove off, after paying for your fuel, without bothering with even a second glance.'

She knew this was true because, like a stupid idiot, she'd watched him go and then spent the rest of the afternoon dwelling on it.

Logan rubbed the back of his neck. 'I'm sorry, but I didn't have time yesterday to—'

She sniffed at his words, not the slightest bit interested in his reasons. No doubt the man figured his life was more important than other people's. 'Well, *I* don't have time now. I need to get to the surgery.'

'Look, yesterday I needed to see my brother. It was important.'

More important than asking after your babies?

The unspoken question sat on the end of her tongue like a stack of foul-tasting copper pennies.

Logan removed his glasses and said, 'I am curious as to why you'd rather not speak to me, though.'

Stunned by his question, she retorted, 'Do me a favour, Dr Fox, and forget we shared a night together. I have.'

'Really?' he asked with disbelief. 'You never think about it—ever?'

She shrugged, not about to admit anything to him. She owed him nothing—especially not the secrets inside her heart. Stupid, useless ones she hated keeping. Secrets she did her best not to acknowledge too often. Secrets she had sworn to one day crush for good.

'It was hardly memorable.'

His whole body stiffened, but he asked, 'Are you saying you—'

With a quick shake of her head, Thurza again moved to go by him. 'I have to get to work. I don't have time to talk to you.'

'I don't understand why you're acting so angry and resentful,' Logan said. 'If anyone should feel peeved, it's me.'

Thurza took a step back at this latest audacity. 'You?'

He nodded and, still keeping his voice low, so no passers-by could hear, said, 'Yes, you're the one who disappeared and left me feeling used the next morning.'

Thurza's mouth fell open at his criticism. Yes, she had left his flat before he'd woken up—but only because she'd been ashamed and uncertain what the etiquette was after a one-night stand. She'd figured he would prefer her gone, to save them both the embarrassment and discomfort of the dreaded morning-after scenario.

'Used? I did no such thing,' she denied hotly.

He raised an eyebrow. 'Oh, I see. You think it's all right for you to use my body for sexual gratification, then sneak out without even a polite thank-you the following morning. I had planned to cook you breakfast.'

'I was being considerate,' she choked, then said mockingly, 'I didn't realise your ego required stroking and bowing to. Were you hoping I would kneel at your feet and thank you kindly for the night?'

'It had nothing to do with my ego,' he dismissed stiffly. 'Surely you can see it's all about good manners.'

'Manners?' Thurza repeated, confused by his attitude. Was there some protocol that nobody talked about concerning casual sex? Some social etiquette she had unknowingly broken by sneaking away?

He nodded in confirmation. 'Yes, good manners.'

Shaking her head, she shifted away from the man and his bewildering complaints, not sure how to respond considering the fact that he'd ignored their sons' existence for so long. Squabbling over manners seemed inconsequential and ridiculous.

'Where are you going?' he asked.

'To work,' she replied.

Where life was normal and no one acted crazy. Where hypocritical males didn't give speeches on politeness when in reality they were guilty of lacking in common decency themselves.

This man had ignored every single letter she'd sent concerning their children, and now he had the two-faced nerve to lecture her on courtesy and manners. Yes, she was going to leave—before she gave in to the unpardonable and deplorable urge to throw that very knowledge right in the man's insolent face. Because a public beach was the last place for that type of confrontation.

'I thought you worked at the garage,' he called after her.

She stopped and turned back to him. 'Not that it's any of your concern, but I have two jobs. One of which I need to get to as I have a patient requiring a blood test in half an hour.'

'But—'

Whatever Logan Fox had intended to say was forgotten when Maddox raced past them without stopping.

'What the...?' Logan's gaze followed Maddox as he headed towards the small building at the far end of the promenade. 'Maddox! What's wrong?'

Although determined to leave, curiosity caused Thurza to wander back to where Logan stood. 'There must be an emergency call. How do you know Maddox?'

Distracted, Logan answered, 'He's my brother.'

'Brother?' she gasped. 'Maddox?'

Logan nodded and pointed to the wooden building his brother and several other people had just disappeared into. 'What *is* that place?'

'It's the lifeboat station,' Thurza answered. 'It's where they store the boat and all the equipment for sea rescues.'

Logan started to walk towards the building, which was more like an oversized beach hut.

'Where are you going?' Thurza asked.

Logan didn't answer straight away, his focus fixed on the small lifeboat as it exited the building and launched into the sea. Finally, he said, 'To see if I can help, of course.'

CHAPTER FOUR

THURZA WALKED AWAY for a second time, intent on not turning back. What Logan chose to do with his time was his business and absolutely not her concern. But her scruples and her medical schooling slowed her footsteps to a drag, and before she could argue with herself she twisted to stare at the sea. Searching the grim horizon, she sighted the lifeboat, bopping on the waves to the east.

What a mess.

What a horrible nightmare of a predicament.

Logan not only remembered her, but he wanted to talk, too. As if they really had anything to say to each other after all this time. Especially as he'd shown no eagerness to converse over the reason why he'd ignored their sons for so long, and she certainly wasn't interested in hearing any excuses.

She sighed and rotated further, until her

gaze fell upon the annoying man who now stood on the beach in front of the lifeboat station. Why did he have to appear, like a huge bad memory, seemingly determined to get reacquainted? Even a selfish jerk would see she wasn't interested. How clear did she have to be? Wasn't pretending not to recognise him a pretty obvious sign? But no, he'd disregarded all said indications and concerned himself only with his own wishes.

Months ago she might have reacted differently—then she would have welcomed his interest. But not after all this time. Eighteen months, for goodness' sake. Where had he been when she'd suffered hours of labour? Had he helped pay for the boys' clothes and a second-hand pushchair when she'd barely been able to pay her bills? No, he'd ignored her letters and carried on with his single, independent and free life.

She closed her eyes, the sting of his rejection still tender and raw. Oh, she hadn't expected flowers and declarations of all-consuming love. But a little respect and a show of interest in the boys hadn't been too much to expect, had it? She certainly hadn't daydreamed romantic visions about them becoming a family, but an acknowledgement of responsibility and support would have meant something—more than the uncaring silence she'd received.

But Logan Fox had offered nothing. He'd stayed out of their lives when she'd needed him. And she refused to let him think he could just walk in and invade it now on—what? A whim?

She'd cried enough useless tears over the man and his heartless dismissal of their sons. On the night she'd given birth to the twins she'd sworn in the darkness, while the boys had been sleeping in their hospital cots, that she'd never shed another tear over him and his rejection.

Dragging her gaze from the male who'd caused so much turmoil in her life, she glanced at her watch. Her patient would be arriving at the surgery soon. The lifeboat crew could deal with the emergency—after all, they were highly trained and capable.

Decision made, she swivelled on the spot and headed towards town. But something stopped her after a few paces, and before she could change her mind again Thurza turned in the direction of the man her instinct warned was trouble and undependable. A man she suspected was set to bring nothing but problems into her life.

* * *

Logan stood on the pebble beach and watched his brother and the rest of the lifeboat team rescue the early-morning swimmer who'd drifted out to sea. The smell of seawater filled his every sense and salt coated his lips like an invisible balm.

A strong wind blew off the choppy grey water, buffeting him and the odd dog walker insane enough to brave a stroll along the beach on such a cold, blustery day. Where only minutes ago he and Thurza had shared an awkward encounter, and where he now stood alone.

Thurza. So much for avoiding her. It seemed that every time he resolved to forget the woman for good, fate pushed her back under his nose. Not that she'd acted any happier over seeing *him*. Their brief conversation had exposed how clearly she would rather he left town and stayed away.

Well, she'd get her wish soon. Two weeks and then he'd be gone—and she could go back to living her life without fear of having to face an ex-inamorato.

The sight of the lifeboat returning halted any further thoughts over Thurza. Letting out a long, relieved sigh, Logan hurried over once the boat hit the shore, the medic inside him desperate to help. Concern for the rescued swimmer and any possible consequences after spending prolonged time in the freezing water crammed his head, and his unease increased when he noted the casualty's advanced age.

'How's he doing?' he asked, as Maddox and another crew member helped the swimmer off the boat. Although a thermal blanket covered his shoulders and torso, violent shaking rocked through the man's body, causing him to stumble as his feet touched the pebbles. 'Has anyone checked him over yet?'

'He's refusing to let us. Insists he's okay,' Maddox answered, his tone making it clear what he thought of the man's reluctance to accept medical help.

Before anyone else could say anything, the man clutched his chest and gasped. 'Pain... My chest...it hurts.'

Logan jumped into action, unconcerned as to whether the lifeboat crew required his expertise. The man needed his help. A speedy diagnosis was all that mattered right now.

'Hello, sir. My name is Logan Fox. I'm a doctor. Let's sit here on the beach for a moment, shall we? It's not very comfortable, but I just want to ask a few questions and check you over.'

Logan, with Maddox's help, carefully lowered the old man down on to the sea-smoothed grey, yellow and white pebbles.

'It's okay,' Maddox assured the other men and women around them. 'My brother really is a doctor and he knows his stuff.'

Logan fixed his whole attention on the swimmer, taking in the blue tinge to his lips and his pale colouring. 'Okay, my friend. I guess you're feeling a little rough, and sitting on these stones probably isn't helping, but we'll soon have you feeling better.'

'Where am I?' the old man wheezed. 'Please…my chest hurts…and my arm.'

Alarm bells rang in Logan's head. Clues and signs immediately clicked together. These symptoms pointed to the probability that the man was suffering a heart attack and possible hypothermia, hence his confusion.

'You're on the beach and…'

Logan sensed movement on the man's other side and glanced up to find Thurza on her knees, staring across at him with concern in her green eyes.

'Need help?' she asked.

Logan nodded, surprised to see her. 'Always welcome, Nurse Bow. I'm pretty certain we're dealing with a—'

Thurza dumped her nurse's bag to one side

and unwound her long woollen scarf, placing it on the pebbles behind the swimmer. Still listening, she addressed the old man. 'Why don't you lie back?' she urged.

Suddenly the swimmer let out a groan and collapsed into unconsciousness. Luckily his head landed in the centre of Thurza's scarf.

'Damn,' Logan swore, immediately placing the casualty into a flat position. 'He's passed out. What's his pulse like?'

Thurza already held the man's wrist. 'Weak, but still there.'

Logan tilted the man's head to clear his airways and check his breathing. 'Okay, my friend... You just relax and let us do our job.'

When no response came from the man, Logan clipped out, 'Right, I suspect our swimmer has suffered a heart attack. Let's start CPR.'

'On it,' Thurza said, placing her hands one on top of the other in the centre of the man's chest, over his breastbone. Her whole attention was focused on their patient.

Maddox crouched at Logan's side and handed him a plastic face shield. Grateful, Logan took it and positioned it over the casualty's mouth. 'Any chance of an AED?'

Maddox lifted a familiar green case containing the requested defibrillator. 'Ambulance is on its way. Anything I can do?'

'Just let Nurse Bow and I do our magic,' he replied, glancing at Thurza. The swimmer's life and care took priority over personal matters, and right now he was grateful for her assistance.

Taking the case from his brother, Logan opened it and switched on the defibrillator. On the other side of the patient Thurza continued to carry out chest compressions, before switching to blow two breaths into the man's mouth.

Someone handed Logan a towel and he quickly dried the swimmer's upper body so he could attach the AED. Left wet, the pads wouldn't stick to him.

Removing two pads from the sealed pack, Logan pulled off the backing paper and fixed each one to the swimmer's chest, then called, 'Move back.'

Both Thurza and Logan leaned away from the casualty, not wanting to interfere with the machine as it analysed the swimmer's heart rhythm. After a few seconds the machine gave them the information they needed.

'No shock required,' Logan stated, moving near again. 'Let's continue CPR.'

Thurza repeated another set of chest compressions. Several long strands of her hair swung around her face as she concentrated on the job of keeping the swimmer alive. After a quick look in Logan's direction, she continued to work with him. They were a team. Neither of them about to give up on the man they were determined to save.

'How long until the ambulance gets here?' Logan asked the group around them, watching them work.

As if his words had conjured up the emergency vehicle, a loud, familiar siren filled the morning air. Logan glanced up to see it slowly making its way along the promenade, avoiding several groups of bystanders observing the action on the beach.

Moments later two paramedics hurried across the pebbles to join them. Logan quickly filled in the pair and then stepped back to allow them to take over. Within minutes they'd transported the swimmer on to a stretcher and into the back of the ambulance. Accompanied by a second whirl of sirens, they drove away.

Letting out a heavy sigh of relief, Logan turned to Thurza. 'Thanks for the help.'

She bent and grabbed her bag and scarf. With a distracted smile, she said, 'You're welcome.'

'Hey, Thurza!' Maddox greeted her brightly

as he joined them. He'd changed out of his foul-weather gear and once more wore everyday clothes. 'How are the twins doing?'

Thurza shot Logan an uncomfortable glance and then looked back at his brother. Her fingers gripped the bag's woven strap tightly before she answered, 'They're fine, thanks.'

Logan's eyes narrowed as she said goodbye and then scurried away. Twins? Thurza had twins? Since when?

Curious, he turned to his brother and asked, 'Thurza Bow has twins?'

Maddox nodded. 'Yeah, sweet babies. Must be nine months old by now. Funny, though... Out of all the women in town, I'd never have pegged Thurza to return home as a single mum after working in the city. Never known her to go on a date or have a boyfriend the whole time I've lived here. Do you know her?'

'We used to work at the same hospital,' Logan said, his gaze following the woman hurrying away from them along the promenade. 'Different departments, but the same building.'

He'd kissed her smart, prickly mouth many times during that one night. Explored her sexy body and captured her seductive moans.

It was the reason he'd found it so hard to push her from his mind for months. Why all his determination to avoid her while in town had evaporated the second he saw her again. Not even the fear of being hit by a meteorite would have moved him from that spot when she'd turned away from the sea and looked up at him.

He rubbed at the collar of his shirt and pushed his glasses further up on to the bridge of his nose. Thurza had infused his memory and his flesh like a recurring infection without any known or effective long-term cure. Not one *he'd* managed to discover, anyway.

All those times he'd seen Thurza walking around St Maria's, something about her had always made him glance twice whenever she'd passed by. But he'd been in a relationship, and dismissed it as nothing but a natural male attraction to a pretty female...

Nine months old? Had Maddox said Thurza's twins were nine months old?

He swallowed as his mind quickly did the maths. Nine months pregnant. Nine months old. Eighteen months since their night together.

His breath hitched hard in his chest while his mind rejected the total he'd arrived at. No way. They couldn't be his. They'd used protection. He'd worn a condom.

Had he checked it afterwards, though? Damn, he couldn't remember. It had been his first one-night stand so he might not have done. But that was basic stuff, surely? He *must* have checked it. He was a doctor, for goodness' sake. Why was he able to recall how her lips tasted, yet not whether the condom they'd used had failed?

Frowning, he forced his rushing mind to slow down and calmly analyse the probability of an unplanned pregnancy. The chance of that night resulting in one would be something like a couple of percent, surely?

She must have met someone else after their night. Someone she hadn't used protection with.

He swallowed again, trying to clear the bitter, uncomfortable taste burning his throat. But it refused to shift. Could Thurza have given birth to his children and then hidden the truth? What was *wrong* with people? Did he carry a sign on his back that stated, *Screw this man over*? Or *Hide the truth from him on every occasion*?

No, he was reading too much into the fact that her children just happened to be nine months old.

But the way she'd wriggled so uneasily when Maddox had asked about her children set off a loud warning in Logan's logical mind. Was fear that he would uncover her secret the real reason why she didn't want to talk to him? Why she acted so offhand and nervous when in his company? Was she terrified he would discover she'd given birth to his children without the courtesy of letting him know? If that was true, then how *dared* she rob him of the chance to be involved?

No. The whole idea was so outrageous and inconceivable it had to be wrong. They'd used a condom.

Yeah, but everyone knew that method of contraception wasn't foolproof, and he had no idea if she had been using any other form of protection against pregnancy.

'Boys or girls?' Logan asked his brother as they left the beach and walked back along the country road towards his brother's property.

'What?'

'Thurza's twins. Boys or girls?'

'Oh, boys,' Maddox answered. 'Are you okay? You look a little sick.'

'I'm fine,' he said, though it was a lie.

No matter how much he wished he could forget the maths, his always sharp mind yelled

that there was a huge chance that, unknowingly, in the past year he had become a father.

And if that was true, what right did Thurza
Bow think she had to keep that news from him?

CHAPTER FIVE

THURZA CLOSED THE front door, glad to be finally home. Her shift at the surgery had dragged after she'd left the beach.

Thanks to Maddox's appearance, she'd succeeded in leaving without further interaction with Logan. Though he still afflicted her thoughts even now, several hours later. When Maddox had enquired after the twins, she'd thought Logan was going to say something. Instead he'd just stared at her with a slightly confused expression. As if the news that she was the mother of twins surprised him. Well, the man might think he could act and pretend ignorance, but she knew better.

And Maddox was his brother!

Did Maddox know Logan was the twins' father?

Had he secretly watched her and reported back to his brother? Had the two of them been secretly plotting and gathering so-called evidence against her?

What evidence, exactly, she didn't know, but the idea angered and unsettled her. Did they stand in judgement, waiting and assessing every single thing she did? Condemn her for working two jobs and not being a stay-at-home mother? Well, she didn't have the luxury of choice—not with two children to feed and clothe.

Staring around the narrow hallway, Thurza absently twisted a plait around her fingertip. The cottage she rented wasn't much, but it was home. A comfortable and safe place she'd created for her family. A place to raise the boys. It wasn't fancy and filled with all the latest gadgets, like the ones she'd noticed in Logan's flat the morning she'd sneaked out, but she loved it. Yes, most of the furniture was second-hand—okay, *all* the furniture. But it was clean and tidy, and after a fresh coat of paint to give it a 'shabby chic' appearance, it looked good. She'd done her best to make it a snug bubble of love for the boys. One she alone had provided. She didn't care if it wasn't extravagant or elegant. It was home. *Their* home.

But now Logan's appearance threatened to upend the serenity she'd worked consistently to provide for her sons since their birth. Demanding her time and reminding her of things she would rather forget.

With a snort, she retrieved the basket full of newly washed baby clothes left on the floor and walked down the hall to the kitchen. Her anger with Logan and the situation she'd spent the last few hours trying to ignore was still cramming her mind above everything else.

When the rattle of the letter box sounded, it barely penetrated her jumbled thoughts. Only when the noise became more insistent did she leave the kitchen and trudge back to the front door.

She cursed silently when she opened it, for not thinking to slip on the chain first. Staring at the man she wished would instantly evaporate on her doorstep, she sighed. 'You, again.'

She saw Logan's gaze move over her body in one long optical sweep. Far too intimately for a man who'd made it very clear he wanted nothing to do with her or their children.

She stiffened and folded her arms. The movement was a mixture of protection and defiance. She had no wish to spend more time in his company, and the sooner he understood that, the better for them both.

Raising an eyebrow, she said, 'Yes?'

'Why don't you tell me about your twin

boys?' Logan demanded, not bothering with pleasant greetings or any explanations as to why he stood, uninvited, outside her home.

Thurza's cheeks warmed when she met his gaze. He was making her feel like a guilty kid, caught doing something naughty. 'Why would I do that?'

Logan stepped closer, the silent battle in his eyes plain to read. 'Because, Thurza Bow, eighteen months ago you and I spent the night together, and now I hear you have nine-month-old twins.'

She swallowed, but refused to back down from the challenge in his gaze. 'So?'

He leaned closer, his eyes once again lowering to run over her, before returning to meet her gaze. 'So I'd really like to know if I'm their daddy.'

I'd really like to know if I'm their daddy?

Thurza tried to resist the reaction slipping through her body both at his intense look and his confrontational puzzling words. Anger? Annoyance? Attraction? Please, no—not the last one. One mistake with this man equalled a forgivable human failing. Two made her a mammoth idiot.

'How dare you turn up at my home and demand answers from me?' she said, tempted to slam the door in his face.

Logan shot her a glare and said, 'I'll happily leave you alone once you answer my question. That's all I want. One answer to one very simple but important question. I'm no Einstein, but the maths I'm doing is adding up to an interesting total. I'll ask you again, Nurse Bow. Are your twin sons also mine?'

She stiffened at his question and at his attitude. If he cared about the boys, why take so long to show any interest in them? No, this whole sudden curiosity about her family smacked of trickery. And why the pretence of not knowing already? It didn't make sense and it increased her misgivings over what game Dr Fox was actually playing by coming here with his demand for answers.

What hidden agenda did he have? And how was it going to impact her and the twins?

She grabbed the door handle, her fingers squeezing around it for support. 'Other than goodbye, Dr Fox, I have nothing to say to you.'

'According to my brother, you have two babies. That might well be my concern. Is it?'

Thurza decided to ignore his question and asked one of her own. 'How did you find out where I live? Did Maddox tell you?'

He shook his head. 'The woman at the cake

shop in town was very helpful when I explained that I'm an old friend of yours.'

She flicked a loose strand of hair away from her face and flashed him her best indifferent expression, determined to distract him from asking further questions about the twins. 'If you're hoping to reconnect for a few hours, then forget it. Some experiences, especially like the one we shared, are best forgotten.'

He tensed at her words and shifted on the doorstep. 'You're still saying that, are you? What's that old saying about the lady protesting too much…?'

Trust the man to be more concerned with a slur on his sexual prowess than with the children he'd supposedly sought her out to discuss. No doubt women usually fawned over him, treating him like a god. Whereas she'd just prefer him to go away and leave her alone.

'Can you even remember that night?' she asked.

She'd learnt a very good lesson after their time together. One she refused to overlook. Mostly never to mix sex with a work crush. Far too messy and disappointing to be worth the resulting turmoil.

'Or are you just confusing me with the nights you've shared with other women?'

He straightened and crossed his arms. 'Just to set you straight, I do not sleep around and I resent the implication that I do.'

'Yeah, right,' she said, not believing him.

She'd grown out of trusting in fairy tales after their liaison. Did he really expect her to believe a man as gorgeous and sexy as he was didn't attract female attention with ease? She'd seen how nurses and doctors swarmed around him like dying bees, desperate for a taste of his own special nectar, when they'd worked at the same hospital. She wasn't the only staff member who'd experienced the hots for him.

Logan took a deep breath and insisted, 'It's true. I do not jump into bed with just anyone. I'm choosy over who I sleep with.'

'You slept with *me*,' she reminded him.

He shocked her by grinning. 'Yes, I did.'

Not sure she wanted to continue with this dangerous diversion in the conversation, she frowned and grabbed the door tighter. 'This conversation is both boring and over. Goodbye, Dr Fox.'

Logan shook his head. 'I'm not leaving until you answer my question,' he insisted. 'I'm staying in town until you give me the information I want. If you wish me to leave then just give me an answer and I'll go.'

'I really don't appreciate your bossy tone,' she complained, stalling.

The spicy scent of his aftershave and the saltiness of the sea clung to his clothes and his body, twirling like an invisible caress through the air, swirling its heady mingled fragrance over her already sensitive nerves and making her all too aware of how close he stood.

'Let's act like grown-ups, shall we?' Logan suggested softly. 'All I want is for you to tell me the truth. Am I the father of your twin sons?'

She lowered her head and sighed, desperate for a break from him and his distracting company. For months she and the boys had happily tootled along, facing each new day with a smile, confident and cheerful in the easy routine they lived by. Now, though, Logan loomed in their lives, threatening that serenity with his questions and demands.

Resigned, she asked, 'You're really not going away until I do, are you?'

He shoved his hands into his trouser pockets and shook his head. 'Nope.'

'What if I don't *want* to answer your questions?' she asked stubbornly.

Her answers had the potential to change

everything she had built since the boys' birth. She lifted her head and unwillingly took in his features. The man was tongue-meltingly good-looking. Not the pretty-boy kind of handsome, but something more honest and real. A fusion between nerdy cool and academic hotness.

'Then I'll stay here until you do,' he warned, staring back at her.

His blue gaze let her know he meant it. He wasn't going anywhere. Not until he had his answers. And then what? What would he do then?

All the frantic concerns of the last two days returned and simmered and gurgled inside her.

Lowering her eyes to his lips, she let her gaze settle there. Her mind became engrossed in the curve of the lower one. Though it looked innocent, Thurza knew how wicked and naughty his mouth could be to a woman's body. How it liked to torture and excite. Tease and please.

Pushing those thoughts away, she reluctantly motioned for Logan to come in, rather than continue their conversation on the doorstep. She showed him into her small sitting room. Lowering himself on to her floral sofa, he looked as out of place as a dirty weathered boulder dropped into an old lady's chintz-and-lace-decorated parlour.

She frowned. 'I don't understand why you keep asking me the question when you already know the answer.'

'But I don't,' he insisted.

'Yes, you do,' she replied. 'I sent several letters to your flat. When you never answered, or contacted me, I figured you didn't want to know. I even visited one day. Your cleaner said you'd gone abroad, and refused to give me any more information or a forwarding address.'

'Ah…' he murmured, suddenly looking uncomfortable. 'I've been working in Malta for over a year. I haven't visited the flat since I left. My cleaner goes in every few weeks to dust and check up on everything. I only recently returned to England, because my…my father died.'

'Your father died?' Thurza asked, reluctant compassion springing awake inside her. She might dislike the man in front of her, but she understood the pain of losing a parent. The way he'd stumbled over the word 'father' pinched at her heart. Grief, no doubt, still overwhelmed him. 'Recently?'

'Ten weeks ago.'

No wonder Logan had travelled to Dorset

to see his brother. He was probably seeking comfort in his sibling's company. As an only child, Thurza had always regretted not having that option. No one person who understood her pain and loss in the same way a brother or sister might have.

She sighed and wrapped her arms around her waist—mostly to stop herself from giving in to the urge to console him with a hug. Losing a parent was hard at any age and any time in a person's life.

'I'm sorry for your loss,' she said.

'Thank you.'

A strange, traitorous warmth, something like hope, floated through her, but she squashed it down flat. Safer to stick to facts and not emotions. The one time she'd behaved the other way around she'd ended up having his children.

'Are you saying you haven't read the letters I sent to your flat?'

He nodded his head in confirmation. 'They must be piled up there. But if you wrote to me, I guess you had a reason to do so.'

Another thought struck Thurza, stopping her from answering. 'If you've never read my letters then why do you think the boys are yours?'

Logan sighed. 'I asked my brother how old your children are.'

'Oh,' she said, before her eyes widened with horror. 'You didn't tell Maddox about our night together, did you?'

'No.'

'Good.' She didn't want anyone to know about their connection until she'd worked out what the man was up to. His explanation of working abroad and not visiting his flat seemed plausible, but she still didn't trust him.

'Are you going to answer my question?' Logan asked, returning her attention to the reason he was in her home. 'I simply want to know if your children are also my children.'

Something inside Thurza twisted at the unexpected expression in his eyes. Was it hope? Yearning? Did he want the answer to be positive? Or was he secretly longing for it to be negative so he could walk away?

Giving in, while wishing she didn't have to, preferring her life to be uncomplicated and straightforward, she forced out the words she doubted anyone had ever used before when dealing with the man in front of her. 'Yes, Logan, they are. You are their father.'

In reply, Logan let out a long, heartfelt sigh. But his expression immediately became closed, giving her no clue to his real feelings on hearing the news.

'What are their names?' he asked.

Thurza hesitated, still reluctant to let him deeper into her private life. But if the man was telling the truth, and he hadn't read her letters, then she couldn't continue to hate him for not getting in touch, could she?

'Tyler and Axel.'

Logan's eyes widened, but he didn't say a word.

She stiffened at his unspoken disapproval of the boys' names—names she'd picked alone, because no one else in her life had cared enough to raise an argument, or pull a face like the one he was doing right now.

'They're lovely names,' she said.

He frowned. 'They're different… When can I meet them?'

She glanced at the clock on the wall, aware they wouldn't be home for hours. 'They're with my aunt and cousin and won't be back until teatime.'

'It must be hard, caring for and providing for two babies,' he remarked after several moments.

She huffed. 'My children are worth it. Look, I have chores to do, so you really need to leave.'

'My name won't be on their birth certifi-cates?' Logan asked suddenly.

Thurza shook her head. 'No, not without your agreement. I sent so many letters in-forming you about my pregnancy and asking you to get in touch. When I didn't receive a reply I figured you didn't want any contact and definitely didn't want to provide towards the boys' upbringing.'

He nodded, but disappointment etched his face, and for the first time in months Thurza suspected she might have judged Dr Logan Fox unfairly.

Perhaps she should have tried harder to get in touch with the man she'd long believed didn't care.

CHAPTER SIX

DID THE FATES get fun out of messing with his life? Logan glared at the moody charcoal sky and dared the rain to increase. How was a man supposed to make a good impression on the mother of his yet-to-be-seen children if he resembled a drowned rat after a hard night partying.

Not that he wished to make *any* impression on Thurza other than in the respectable father stakes. He certainly wasn't hoping to rekindle the flare of attraction that had led to their night together. A night she'd lied about not enjoying.

He remembered how her body had sung and sighed beneath his fingertips. Oh, yes, Thurza lied, indeed. Each word nothing but a forgery. What he'd yet to understand was why.

Removing his glasses, he rubbed away the rain spots with a handkerchief before putting them back on. His vision was now less spotted, but his thoughts were still focused on Thurza.

Just stop with the musings, Fox. You're here to meet her from work—not fantasise about her pretty body or the sweet noises she makes when aroused.

The less he reflected on that the quicker his mind would settle on the important stuff—like their children. They were all that concerned him...all that mattered in his life.

The maddening woman who'd unknowingly haunted his days for over a year had now given him the ideal opportunity to exorcise her from his head for good. The twins were one thing, but his craving for Thurza was a separate issue. One he intended to rid himself of completely. If they spent time together it was bound to happen. Familiarity bred contempt and all that. Once they got to know one another properly she'd become just another woman. The mother of his sons and nothing else. A friend for life—or at least until the boys turned eighteen and could make their own decisions with regard to seeing and spending time with him.

'Hello.'

Startled out of his ponderings, Logan stared at Thurza, instantly noting the wariness lining her face. A feeling he guessed had arisen from his unexpected appearance outside the doctor's surgery.

He hated witnessing it. Somehow they needed to resolve things between them so they could build an amicable relationship. A relationship for the boys' sake, and absolutely nothing to do with rekindling anything between them. The past couldn't be changed, but the future—theirs and their sons'—would be simpler if they kept everything platonic, set aside any remaining physical desire and concentrated only on the two babies they'd created.

'Hi—' His normally deep voice had shifted skywards in its pitch. Gulping, he tried again, hoping for the return of his usual baritone. After a sharp cough, he croaked, 'All finished?'

'Yes. You?'

Logan nodded. He'd applied to work as a locum at the same surgery after seeing an advert online. Today he'd worked his first morning shift, and had thought he'd take advantage of their same finishing time.

Thurza frowned and shifted her handbag further on to her shoulder. The guardedness in her green gaze had turned to full-on distrust. 'Is there something you want, Dr Fox?'

'Logan,' he corrected. He'd imagined her pleasure at his appearance when she came out, not this uneasy awkwardness. 'I thought I'd walk you home.'

She tilted her head and studied him with the same intensity he might allot to a complicated medical case. Unspoken worries clouded her anxious eyes and her caginess increased.

'Why?'

A perfectly reasonable query, and one he unfortunately had no logical answer for. He'd stood waiting in the rain because his thoughts continually circled around this woman and how to make things right between them. He and Thurza had created a family, yet they hardly knew each other. Where did they go from here? How did they create a stable relationship in which they could both raise their children?

He didn't want to start pushing into her life, throwing his opinion around like a boxer throwing sharp jabs. But he also refused to stand on the side like an undesirable family member, grateful for any crumb tossed in his direction. He was a father, and he longed to be a good one. And that meant being involved in his children's lives.

Thurza started walking out of the surgery

car park. 'You don't need to. I've managed to find my way home many times without help. I have my own internal satnav.'

'I thought...' Logan began. What? That after one conversation they would be able to put the past to rest? That Thurza would accept his excuses for not being involved with their children sooner and become his best friend overnight?

Not going to happen when he suspected she still viewed him as the kind of man who walked away from his responsibilities and shirked his duties. Even though the truth was the opposite. If he'd known about the boys he would never have left England and stayed away. He would have shadowed her, every step of the pregnancy, and offered his help and support any time she'd requested it.

When he'd seen Thurza that night at the bar he'd recently called off his six-month engagement. Despite liking his fiancée, he'd come to realise that *liking* someone didn't make him eager to slip a gold band on her finger and utter the words *I do*. He'd realised he didn't love the woman. Not the way she deserved to be loved. The terrible truth was that he'd seen their union as a relationship based on family friendship, cold rationality and desperation. A marriage to please others, with little thought for himself or his needs.

His ex-fiancée was perfect—clever and beautiful. But take away the friendship and Logan had come to see there was little else. No deep soul connection or solid bond. No heart-thudding attraction.

The feelings and desire between them just hadn't been strong enough. Not in the way Valentine's cards declared they should be. Or in the way romantic films dramatised them. It had been just an empty relationship formed between two people who had seen time passing without having ticked the marriage box. A decision based on common sense instead of that mystical sentiment called love.

They'd drifted into a relationship—one that had never felt right—because everyone had told them it was a good match. Not really understanding the relationship thing, for a while Logan had figured if two people got on and had similar interests it would be enough for a marriage. But as the weeks had gone by a voice in his heart had kept insisting he was wrong.

So he'd ended the engagement and then he'd seen Thurza that night, laughing with a group of friends, and for the first time in his life something concerning a woman had felt right. He'd craved it. He'd given in to his self-ish hunger to be with her. He'd hankered for a pair of warm arms to find comfort in and hide from the mess of his life, and Thurza was the woman who had provided them. That part he didn't regret. His passionate, wonderful night with Thurza was worth everything.

'I thought we could get to know each other a little better,' he explained now. They had to start somewhere, otherwise they'd be raising the boys in silence and polite disquiet.

Thurza hesitated, confirming his fears that her opinion of him hung around ground level.

'I think I know enough concerning you, thanks,' she said.

Shaking his head, he stepped into her path. 'No, you don't. That's the problem we have, isn't it? I don't blame you for thinking badly of me for not contacting you—though I truly didn't know about your pregnancy. If I had, I swear things would have been different. But none of that is important right now. You and I have created twin sons, and I hope you might try and see that we need to come to some kind of truce and learn to get along. Despite what you might think, I don't regret our night to-gether.'

'You don't?' she asked. 'Even though the

twins are the result of it? Babies you didn't plan on becoming a father to?'

He shook his head, sending the raindrops clinging to the ends of his hair flying. 'No regrets at all, Thurza. So may I walk you home?'

He waited for her decision, determined not to give any hint of the eagerness running through him. She needed to learn to trust him, and he sensed it would take time. Thurza's misgivings were completely understandable, and only time and patience would banish them.

She shrugged and then, like a Viking queen bestowing a rare honour on a mere Christian mortal grovelling at her majestic feet, said, 'I suppose so. If you really wish to.'

Keen to accept the offer, despite her grudging agreement, Logan walked at her side, searching his mind for a safe subject to start a conversation with. Again, the unwelcome notion of raising the boys in silence came to him.

'Tell me something few people know about you, Thurza Bow.'

She hesitated for a moment, before answering, 'My family has lived in this town since the seventeen hundreds.'

He shot her a glance and raised an eyebrow. 'Long time to stay in one place.'

She nodded and smiled. 'Yes, it is.'

Logan tugged up the zip on his jacket. 'Thurza's an unusual name. Does it have local origins?'

'No. My father named me after a great-great-grandmother. She raised thirteen children and ran a business with her husband.'

He grinned. 'Not selling early forms of contraception, I'm guessing?'

She laughed and shook her head, stepping to one side as an elderly couple passed them. 'No. Fish.'

'Fish?' he repeated.

Thurza smiled and nodded towards the bay in the distance. The glistening water and the end of the pier were visible from where they stood. 'They lived near the sea. What else would they sell?'

'Do you hope for more children?' Logan asked, picturing the woman walking at his side in the centre of a family of infants.

He found he liked the image. He'd never really experienced a close and loving family. Any real show of affection had stopped after his mother had passed away. Victor had always been too busy with his business deals to care about Logan's emotional requirements.

'The two babies I have already keep me busy, thanks.'

He nodded and glanced her way. 'Two I've yet to meet.'

For a few moments they walked in comfortable silence. Strange… Generally people liked to fill quiet moments with words and noise, yet Thurza appeared content to just walk beside him. As if they were a couple who'd known each other for years instead of the loose acquaintances they really were.

'What are they like?' he finally asked, breaking the silence.

He'd asked Maddox the same question, but he'd just said they looked like all babies—not much hair and lots of dribble. He hadn't pushed for more information, not wanting to raise his brother's curiosity. He'd tell him later on…once he got used to the notion of being a father.

Logan tried to picture each baby. Were they identical twins or not? Did they favour their mother's fair complexion? Or perhaps they'd inherited his darker colouring? Black hair like his, or blonde like Thurza's? What eye colour did they have? Green? Blue? One of each?

'Who?' Thurza asked.

'Our sons,' he answered, and then repeated, 'What are they like?'

'Wonderful,' she replied, her face softening with love.

A flash of jealousy shot through him. One that both shocked and embarrassed him. He couldn't blame her for the fact he'd left the country and missed the chance to know about her pregnancy and meet his own children. She'd tried to give him the opportunity, but he'd run away from his life in England. He had not been willing to deal with Victor's anger and disappointment over his broken engagement...with his guilt over hurting a friend and his unanticipated surge of feeling towards Thurza after their brief hours together.

Without leaving an address for his post to be forwarded to, he'd closed off all opportunity for things to turn out differently between them. And while he'd left behind his old life she had grown two new ones, and experienced nausea and joy in doing so. Through his own actions, he'd missed out on it all.

Thurza owned those memories of her pregnancy and the boys' early days. They were hers alone. While he had tended the medical needs of strangers, she'd witnessed their sons' developmental firsts. Their first yawn, their first smile. Even their first dirty nappies. He'd missed it all. Every last thing. He envied her that time and experience.

'Why did you leave St Maria's?' he asked, curious as to why she'd returned to this town during her pregnancy. What had brought her back here after living in the city? From what he'd seen it was just like every other seaside town, only smaller.

Thurza stilled, fiddling with the pink scarf around her neck. 'My cousin and her parents are here.'

'What about your own parents?'

She shook her head and glanced away. 'My father died when I was seventeen and my mother remarried not long after. She lives in France now. She wanted me to go with her, but our relationship became tense after my father's death, so I stayed and moved in with my aunt and uncle. I came back here because I was pregnant and alone and this town is home. It's where I belong.'

Home. The way she uttered the modest word revealed how special and important this place was to her. Between boarding school and university, Logan had never felt any real connection to a place. He'd always been able to adapt to his surroundings wherever they were. Especially after his mother's death, when the big house in Salisbury had lost the little warmth she'd created with the scent of her Italian cooking and the rowdy songs she'd loved to sing.

The rain started to increase. Thurza pulled a red-and-white-spotted umbrella from her handbag. She didn't speak again until she'd opened it and lifted it over their heads.

Noting the height difference between them, she offered him the handle with a wry smile. 'Here, you'd better hold it. I'd hate to accidentally give you bruises or stab your eyes out.'

Logan reached for the handle, their hands brushing as he took it from her. Heat zoomed into his fingers and along his arms, reminding him of all the reasons a platonic relationship between them made sense and why he shouldn't want to change that. But his mouth had dried at the contact, and flashes of their night together pitched through his mind. Tantalising shadowy reminders of those passion-filled hours.

His gaze flicked to her face and then her lips. Pretty pink lips that he suddenly yearned to kiss, to see if she tasted as good as he recalled. But that would be a mistake. And this time he was determined, when dealing with this woman, that he would listen to his brain and not other unreliable parts of his body.

Romance of any kind had no place in this

relationship. And that was the rational, level-headed decision he intended to stick to, no matter how much his body wished otherwise.

Thurza slowed to a stop outside a small farm-house with a thatched roof. A huge hanging basket packed with variegated ivy and orange pansies hung by the pink front door. Fortunately, the rain had eased, and now only heavy sullen-looking clouds filled the sky.

'Why have we stopped?' Logan asked curiously.

He recognised the road as the same one his brother lived on. Though Maddox's rambling farmhouse dwarfed this tiny cottage easily. The building's simple and somewhat crude architecture indicated that it was probably one of the original houses in the area.

'This is where my cousin Rachel lives,' Thurza replied. 'The boys are here. I won't be long.'

Moving away, she'd almost disappeared around the tall privet hedge surrounding the property before Logan reached out and stopped her. Gently easing her backwards, he asked, 'Shall I come with you?'

Clearly startled by his suggestion, Thurza struggled not to show her lack of enthusiasm for the idea. Then, with a sharp but decisive shake of her head, she said, 'It's best if you stay here. I'll run in and grab the boys. Be out in a few minutes. Five at the most. Honestly, I won't be long. Why don't you shelter behind this nice thick hedge and wait? Yes, that's a good idea. Just stay here.'

Firmly manoeuvring Logan backwards, she practically shoved him into the large shrub before hurrying off in the direction of the cottage, the heels of her shoes echoing in the quiet air.

Stunned, Logan straightened and tried to make sense of Thurza's actions. Anyone would think she preferred to hide him from both the house and the person inside. Was she ashamed of him? Did she not want her cousin to see them together? Perhaps she hoped to keep him as some sort of dirty secret?

Straightening, Logan pushed his shoulders back and stretched his neck. He refused to be hidden away. The whole idea that they'd done something wrong or shameful burnt like caustic liquid. Was that how she saw their night together? Their sons?

Marching to the end of the hedge, he peeked round the dense vegetation, nearly stabbing his nose on a sharp twig that was sticking out. Narrowing his eyes, he considered his options. If he stopped hiding and instead waited on the doorstep would Thurza open the door and pretend to her cousin that she didn't know him, the way she had when they'd bumped into each other the other morning on the beach? Or would she slam the door in his face and rush out through the rear entrance?

He was tempted to march up the path and plant himself on the doorstep just to find out. But he wouldn't, because he didn't plan on upsetting Thurza and he wouldn't have any rights until his name was put on the boys' birth certificates. And the last thing he was going to suggest now was having a DNA test carried out to prove his paternity. Not yet— if ever.

He sought to become Thurza's friend, not her enemy. Although perhaps it wasn't him she was concerned about, but her cousin's reaction. How bad could this Rachel be? From what little Thurza had said, it was obvious the two women were close. But did that mean the woman interfered in Thurza's life? Or maybe someone else was inside with the cousin? Someone Thurza didn't want him to meet?

Of course, her family must all hate him for leaving Thurza to cope with her pregnancy and the twins' arrival alone. Was she concerned about their response to him? What if she had painted him as so bad and inconsiderate that she was now worried about her family's reaction to his unexpected arrival?

Or was there a man Thurza would rather didn't learn that Logan was in town? Someone she was dating? Maddox didn't know her well enough to know if she was or wasn't seeing someone, did he?

A noise from the house drew Logan out of his deliberations. Shifting back out of sight, thanks to a thin patch in the evergreen bush's growth, he viewed the cottage's front entrance.

Thurza stood in the open doorway, manoeuvring a black double buggy over the threshold. Two baby boys, dressed in matching blue-and-red Fair Isle patterned hats and blue snowsuits, leaned forward in their seats as she pushed the buggy over the wide stone step and on to the gravel path.

Logan's heart stalled at the sight of the two small identical faces and the dark hair poking out from beneath the rims of each hat—the same shade as his own, from what he could tell. Chubby cheeks and matching mischievous sweet smiles sent his heart melting into a puddle of gooey, manly father love.

These angelic babies were his children. His sons. His true family members. Other than

Maddox, they were his only real family in the whole world.

Swallowing hard to dislodge the sudden thick lump in his throat, he continued to take them in. These two small human beings were his babies and no one could steal that fact from him. Or deny it. Because even with a few feet between them he could see those faces were small images of his own. His very own little family.

Oh, dear God, look what he'd done! Times two.

A surge of overwhelming emotion gripped him and refused to loosen its unrelenting grasp. He couldn't be a father. Not now, not ever. A doctor and an ex-son, yes. An ex-fiancé, come to that. No matter how he viewed it, he always ended up being an ex-something. But a father? No, he didn't want to fail in this and become an ex-daddy, too.

His life had always centred around medicine and achievement. Helping people with their illnesses and physical problems. But a father? The dreams he and Victor had concocted over the years had never included two boys with adorable heart-shaped faces and kissable plump baby cheeks.

Wiping at the sudden moisture in his eyes, he stepped away to steady his breathing.

Grasping the prickly hedge to steady his wobbly legs and keep himself upright, he stopped trying to hold back the sentiments the sight of these two small boys had instantly sparked in his heart. A heart he'd secretly feared too battered to react. But thankfully it had. He truly was a father. Not just in words or in hope. He was a dad to two flesh-and-blood children. His very own sons.

Logan's gaze met Thurza's as she and the pushchair appeared around the hedge, and he struggled between wanting to grab her in a big hug and scatter kisses all over her face or being furious with the fates for denying him his children from the very beginning of their precious lives.

He let go of the bush and then crouched beside the pushchair, coming face to face with his boys. His and Thurza's. The babies they had created together. And now he'd seen them he refused to be one of those fathers who said hi and then bye. It didn't matter what his panicked inner voice said. These little boys deserved the best of fathers and he promised to be that, no matter what.

He would never throw their love away as though it was nothing. The way his father had his. He would take these boys' hands and guide them and love them.

With resolve calming his thoughts he drew in a determined breath. For the next eighteen years he and Thurza would share the connection of their sons and do it civilly and respectfully. Working together as friends, not rivals. No way would he walk away and ignore the twins' existence. These boys were his and he was theirs for the rest of his days.

God, they were cute.

Thurza stepped forward and expertly undid the clasp surrounding the child next to her. Lifting her son into her arms, she spoke softly to him, before turning to face Logan. 'This is Axel.'

Unable to resist the pull any longer, Logan touched the boy's arm. His fingers were shaking as they stroked over the material of the snowsuit. 'Hey, there, little man. How's it going?'

Thurza snuggled Axel and grinned. 'He's a bundle of mischief and trouble. I swear he'll be an explorer when he's older.'

A disgruntled squawk from the pushchair drew their attention downward. This time Logan undid the strap, his fingers fumbling over the simple task until finally he managed to move the sections apart and pull his son into his arms.

'Hey, there, little man number two. How are you doing? You must be Tyler.'

'That's right,' Thurza said. 'And this young man is mostly content to let his brother get into mishaps alone and play with his toys instead. But don't be fooled. He's just as much of a rascal as his twin brother—just a little less rowdy while being so.'

The baby reached out and grabbed Logan's face, diving forward to bite his nose.

'Tyler, no,' Thurza scolded gently, putting her hand between her son's mouth and Logan's nose. 'Be nice to…'

'Daddy,' Logan supplied swiftly, determined to start his relationship with his children with the complete truth and nothing else. No relegating him to his first name or some pretend title of 'uncle'—not even for a short time. He never wanted the boys to doubt his commitment to them. Now he knew about their existence he wasn't going away. And it was best that everyone, especially their mother, understood that.

'Daddy,' Thurza repeated softly. After a moment, she offered, 'Why don't you come back to our house and spend the afternoon getting used to your new role?'

Logan grinned at the child in his arms, pleased that Thurza had made the offer so willingly. Placing his palm nervously against Tyler's soft cheek, he said, 'Sounds great. What do you think, Tyler? Do you want your daddy to come over and play?'

Tyler giggled and gave Logan a bright smile that melted his heart all over again.

'I think that's a yes,' Thurza murmured gently.

CHAPTER SEVEN

'JUST PUT AXEL in the playpen,' Thurza directed, moments after they'd entered her cottage.

Slipping off her red coat and her scarf, she hung both on the hall stand, indicating for Logan to do the same with his brown leather jacket. With a quick smile, she disappeared into the kitchen.

Logan watched her go before turning his attention to the baby in his arms. Baby shampoo and another scent drifted around him as he cradled his son to his side. It was an aroma completely unique to small babies and reminded him of pure, unadulterated sweetness and wholesome innocence.

This infant and his twin brother depended on Thurza for everything. For too long they had been Thurza's sole concern, from the day she'd discovered she was expecting them. Had she cried over their existence the way his mother supposedly had? Regretted the predicament she'd found herself in?

How she must have hated him for not being around to support them all…for leaving her to face a future without the boost of his financial and emotional support. How had she managed to afford everything two babies required? Even basic baby paraphernalia added up, without multiplying it by two.

And how had she survived the endless sleepless nights every new parent talked about with resigned loving dread. Weeks and weeks of constantly tending to two babies' needs. Caring for one almost broke most new parents during the first tough weeks and months of their child's life—but two? And doing it all alone with no one to lean on except her cousin Rachel.

Logan shook his head in awe and smiled at his son. Thurza Bow must be one strong woman. Not only beautiful, but capable, too.

A sharp squeal from Tyler, still strapped in the pushchair, penetrated Logan's thoughts. Setting Axel down into the large playpen that occupied a good portion of the lounge floor, he turned to give Tyler the attention he demanded.

'Hey, there, buddy boy,' Logan murmured softly as he cradled his second son in his arms, loving the unaccustomed huggable weight of his child pressed into his hip.

Despite being a completely new feeling, it felt comforting and right. A perfect match. An absent piece he hadn't even recognised was missing now returned to its right place.

'I'm your daddy and I'm very happy to be so. It's important you understand how much.'

'Are you?' a voice asked from behind them.

Logan spun round and smiled at Thurza, who stood in the doorway. Her hair now sat in a messy bundle at the back of her head and she wore a purple apron over faded well-washed jeans and a cream jumper. While he and the boys had been getting acquainted, she'd changed out of her work uniform and into everyday home clothes.

With no reason to lie, he nodded. 'Yes. I'm very happy.'

She seemed pleased by his answer and, with a sharp nod in return, said, 'Good.'

'When you first realised you were pregnant,' he asked, eager to know, even though he risked not liking her answer, 'were you upset?'

The question came out awkward and blunt, but it was too late to soften it. Until he'd actually uttered the words he hadn't realised how important her answer was to him. He hated

the idea of the unplanned pregnancy being
something she regretted. An event in her life
she would change if given the chance. Oh, she
loved the boys now—he could see that—but
back then had she cursed the failure of the
contraception they'd used? Had she blamed
and resented him?

Thurza folded her arms and frowned. 'No,
I was worried at first, about how I would
cope, but when I got used to it, I was happy.'

Relief and lightness extinguished his private fears. No regrets or heartache for this
woman, then. No tears cried over the con-
ception of their children. No secret disappointments. Nothing she wished could be
changed. No, she'd wanted their sons, and
the knowledge filled him with a strange and
unexpected joy.

'You were? Really?'

She smiled. 'Yes—very happy.'

Pleasure at her honesty warmed and thawed
his heart, soaking into areas he'd believed
dead and frozen after Victor's death. 'You
weren't angry?'

'No,' she said, slipping her hands into the
apron's large front pocket. 'I guess the universe figured my life required a double shaking up.'

He smiled. 'Yeah, mine, too. I just wish…'

'Yes?' she probed, lifting her chin a couple of inches higher as she waited for him to continue.

The self-conscious movement indicated that she anticipated some form of criticism or disapproval from him. Thurza might be amazing in the mother stakes, but it was clear after their dealings over the last few days that the woman still questioned his motives and was reluctant to wholly let go of her undercurrent of suspicion in regard to him. It was as though she expected him to say or do something unkind or critical.

Glancing at the baby in his arms, he went on, 'I just wish that I'd helped you from the start...through the pregnancy and everything. All those days and weeks I missed out on.'

She chuckled softly and admitted, 'Well, it's a good thing you did miss some bits. Morning sickness—yuck! I suffered a full three and a half months of it. All day long. I doubt you'd have wanted much part of that.'

'Bad? I'm sorry you had to go through that alone.'

'Horrendous,' she admitted. 'And from the fifth month I took on the appearance of a large house, minus the chimneys. Mind, if you'd turned me on my head you may not have thought so. I'm sure in a low light and from afar my legs could easily have resembled two Victorian chimney pots.'

'I bet you looked beautiful,' Logan said, not believing her. Thurza's natural beauty would have been enhanced during pregnancy.

The idea of her swollen with his children stirred something primitive. Something he figured was best kept to himself. Otherwise he had a feeling he'd be marched back out through the door for daring to utter it.

'Only someone who never saw me would say so,' Thurza declared. 'My cousin insisted I stay away from zoos in case the elephants mistook me for one of their own and I triggered a stampede.'

He chuckled and pushed his glasses up on to the bridge of his nose. 'I think you're exaggerating.'

She sighed heavily and shook her head. 'I'm not. I was truly huge. Mammoth, even. People crossed the street when I went out, for fear of getting knocked over by my baby bump as they moved past me.'

He looked once again at Tyler, who seemed happy to stare back at him. His eyes were blue, just like Logan's. Curiosity twinkled in their depths. Warm, instant love for the infant seeped from his heart. This young boy was his son. *His.* It still felt like a dream. A good dream. No, better than that. A fantastic dream. One he never wanted to disappear, lose or wake up from.

With a self-conscious cough, he glanced back at Thurza. 'How did you manage?'

She shrugged and blew a loose strand of hair that had fallen from the hair clasp back from her face. 'I just did. I concentrated on these two babies I had to care for and provide for. Taking it a day at a time. I simply did my best. What other choice did I have?'

'I'm sorry I left,' he said, meaning his words. 'If I'd realised the condom had failed I would never have—'

'It's in the past,' she said, with a dismissive wave of her hand. Her tone suggested she didn't hold any grudge against him now she knew the reason why he'd never contacted her. 'No point fretting over what's done and gone.'

Logan agreed, but if destiny had tapped him on the shoulder right that minute and offered him the chance to travel in time, back to when Thurza had first discovered her pregnancy, he'd have grasped hold of it and agreed to any condition or clause issued, just to experience every step with her. To be able to hold her hand during those hours while she gave birth. To cradle his sons in his arms moments after they'd taken their first breath. To thank Thurza for the gift she'd given him on the day she did it.

But wishing for the impossible was a waste of hope and time, just as Thurza had said. All he could do was help from today onwards. Be a father in the way no man had ever bothered to be to him. A good father. A loving father who'd make the winners of those 'Father of the Year' competitions look like bumbling amateurs. Bestow upon his sons a sincere and honest love and endless affection.

Logan watched Thurza disappear back to the kitchen, a trace of regret and disappointment still lingering in his soul. He'd left her with no choice but to survive and bring their children into the world alone, while he'd run off hoping to forget the muddle he'd made of his own life. A state *he'd* caused by believing he could organise and control everything—including getting engaged to a woman he didn't love.

What a fool he was. Life and fate couldn't be controlled or manipulated. Neither could people and relationships. Both deserved better attention than he'd given either one.

No wonder his engagement had ended in chaos and bad feeling. Long-time family friendships had been stained forever by his thoughtlessness and actions. Life couldn't be placed into neat squares that suited only him and his requirements. He'd given a ring to the wrong woman, when he should have waited for his own 'special one' to step into his world.

He wasn't like his elderly patient Matthew back in Malta. He didn't need to fill his days and years with 'almost perfect' women to pass the time. Thank God he'd understood that before he'd walked down the aisle to 'The Wedding March'.

But right at this moment the sour taste of remorse coated his conscience. A feeling far more potent and disappointing than any shame over his botched engagement. Unknowingly, the decisions he'd taken back then had caused him to fail three very important people. Thurza, Axel and Tyler.

Because he had a horrible feeling that when he'd left England all those long months ago he'd walked away from the one woman who might have become his own 'special one'.

And he'd stayed away too long to ever know if that could have been true.

After a late lunch, Logan followed Thurza out into the back garden. The autumn sun was for once warm enough to enjoy. Carrying their mugs of tea and a plastic container of mini chocolate muffins outside, they headed to the floral swing seat at the end of the garden.

With full tummies, the twins had fallen asleep in their high chairs, and were now both stretched out in their matching light blue cots for an afternoon nap.

Joining Thurza on the seat, Logan kept a respectable gap between them. Without the twins to distract them, this was the perfect opportunity for getting to know each other better and discussing the twins. No disruptions, no babies, no patients to tend—just the two of them.

Logan settled back, glancing briefly at the woman beside him. Thurza intrigued him. The woman was beautiful, so it was no great mystery how they'd ended up making love. But she possessed more than just sex appeal. She was straight-talking, honest and seemingly not impressed by him at all—she fascinated him.

He'd never struggled to attract female attention, but this woman acted as though she viewed him as just another man in the world—and, strangely, he found he hated it. Although he had no plans to form anything with her other than a relationship shaped around and solely for their children. A family circle, but not living together as involved partners who were in love with each other, but as friends.

Unfortunately, his stupid inner male kept envisaging the idea of something more. Something he was adamant would never happen. He refused to ruin things between them because he couldn't control his sex drive.

Dragging the heel of his shoe along the grass and through a thick trail of spilt sand from the red plastic sandpit shaped like a clam, he half turned towards her. His eyes ran over her hair and face, stopping at the curve of her neck. 'I want to apologise again.'

She raised an eyebrow and enquired, 'What for?'

He twisted fully on the seat until he faced her. 'For not being around during your pregnancy and the birth. I failed you by not contacting you to double-check there were no repercussions from that night. It was a mistake. And it's no excuse, but I am sorry.'

'I never gave you my phone number,' she pointed out, taking a sip of her tea. 'All I had was your address.'

Logan took a gulp of his own drink. The tea was just the way he preferred it. Strong and sugarless. Resting the green mug on his leg, he asked, 'Why did you leave that morning before I woke up?'

It had bothered him at the time, making him wonder if he'd done something wrong during that night. Something that had left her uncomfortable and caused her to leave without a word. Or perhaps he'd said something thoughtless and upset her?

'Why did you sneak out? Did I do something to offend you, or…?'

'Is that what you think?' she asked with surprise.

He shrugged, still not sure, just conscious of how it had left him feeling. As if he'd failed or messed up in some way.

'I thought…' His words trailed off. Secretly, a stupid part of him had imagined that they would wake up the next morning and spend the day together. Get to know one another a little bit better.

'Logan?' she coaxed.

He sighed and admitted, 'Look, I don't know what I thought—but I meant what I said the other day. I would have made you breakfast, at least. I certainly would have satisfied your hunger.'

Her green gaze searched his face and one corner of her mouth twitched. 'Truly?'

'Food hunger, that is. Not—' He broke off,

seeing that his words could be taken another way. 'Yes.'

Ripping the top off the plastic container, she offered him a chocolate muffin. 'Did I really make you feel used?'

He took a muffin, glancing away for a second before answering, 'Yes, I guess you did. I know some men might not care much over spending a night with a woman, but I'd never... You were... Hell, Thurza, you were the first woman I'd ever shared a night with in that way. It's not who I am. Yes, I've had lovers, but I don't sleep around with just anyone.'

She smiled softly, as though his admission pleased her. Shyly, she reached out and touched his chin, her fingers fluttering over his skin lightly like a fairy's footsteps. 'Good, because if we're confessing soul-wrenching truths, then you should know that I had never spent a night like that with a man either. You were my first and I suspect my last one-night encounter. I was just as much a novice as you. And the reason I left before you woke up was because I was embarrassed, and I'd heard other women say that men hated the unease and gaucheness of the following morning, so I thought I was doing the right thing by going.'

He chuckled and captured her hand, rubbing his thumb lightly over her skin. 'I wish you'd stayed.'

She tilted her head, her eyes thoughtful. 'You do?'

He smiled, conscious of her long, elegant fingers against his own. The touch and connection was totally innocent, yet heat warmed his cheeks and he feared he was blushing like a stupid kid.

'We're a pair, aren't we?' he mused, lowering their joined hands until they rested on the cushioned seat between them.

He was secretly relieved when she didn't pull away from his hold or tell him to let go. He liked the feel of her hand in his. Just as when he'd held the twins, it felt as though it belonged there. And friends could touch, couldn't they? As long as they didn't go any further. And they wouldn't.

She smiled, lifting her mug to take another sip of her drink. 'We seem to be. May I ask you a personal question?'

'Yes.'

'Why did you leave St Maria's? I recall hearing rumours about a failed relationship or something concerning a woman.'

His heart twisted, but he wasn't overly surprised by the question. Hospitals were a hotbed of gossip and rumour, so it was only natural she would have heard about it after he'd left England. He just wished he didn't have to admit to being such a fool.

'I was engaged for a short time,' he said. 'Six months.'

'Engaged?' Thurza echoed.

He nodded, before confessing, 'To a woman I didn't really love.'

'You didn't?' she repeated. 'Why not?'

'Because for a long while I mistook close friendship for love. We'd been friends since we were children and our families were keen on the match. But as soon as people started to talk about the wedding I realised that it wasn't what I wanted. It was all my fault, and my ex-fiancée is a lovely woman who thankfully has moved on. I hear she's happy with a new man. They plan to marry next year, I believe. Though I doubt I'll be invited to the wedding. Nor should I be.'

'Oh…' Thurza said thoughtfully. 'No regrets?'

'Only that I hurt and embarrassed her in front of our families and friends. She deserved better from me. It was disrespectful.'

She nodded and remarked, 'It would have been worse if you'd married her and only understood your true feelings after the confetti had dropped out of your hair.'

'You're right,' he agreed, deciding they'd talked enough about the past. Where relationships were concerned, the last couple of years had not been his greatest triumph. He squeezed her hand, glad once more that she didn't break the connection, and said, 'You and I need to get to know one another better. For Tyler's and Axel's sake, of course.'

Thurza shifted on the padded seat. An unexpected twinkle of mischief was brightening her eyes, turning them from their usual sea green to almost jade. 'How well do you want to know me, Logan Fox? So well you can tell what I'm thinking?'

'Yes,' he answered immediately.

The notion of discovering her intimate thoughts and desires suddenly intrigued him. What did she really think of their situation? Of him? Did she like him any better than she had yesterday? Or was she still undecided as to whether to let him into her family fully? Perhaps she figured he would eventually grow bored? Fade into the background and rarely visit? He hoped she wasn't clinging to the latter, because she'd be disappointed. He intended to stay right here in town until they'd settled things between them and he'd got to know his children.

'Why?' she asked.

'Because we should try to get along,' he replied. He was determined to prove they could deal maturely with both the circumstances and each other. 'Don't you think?'

Her eyes became serious and held his. 'Do you know what I'm thinking right now?'

He scanned her face, searching for hints or clues, a telling shadow of her thoughts. After a few seconds, he admitted, 'I have no idea, but I wish I did.'

Without another word, she leaned back and closed her eyes, a faint smile playing around her mouth. Her silence signified that whatever her thoughts were, she meant to keep them to herself…tease him with the unknown.

Pushing the seat into a gentle rocking motion, she offered, 'I have the evening off. Would you like to stay for dinner? It won't be anything fancy, but it will be edible.'

'I'd love to,' he replied, searching her face again for the smallest inkling as to her thoughts. The woman appeared nothing but serene and relaxed.

'Tell me about your cousin,' he said, eager to keep their conversation going.

Thurza opened her eyes and frowned. 'Rachel?'

He nodded. 'You're close?'

'Very. She's extremely bossy, and loves to

tell me how to live my life, but we grew up and lived together after my father died, when my aunt and uncle offered me a home.'

Logan wavered between curiosity and respect for her privacy. Was it too soon for sharing further personal information? But, then again, she had asked about his engagement. Finally, simple nosiness won over tact.

'How exactly did your father die?'

Thurza let out a soft, sad sigh that expressed more than any words could. Suddenly he regretted asking, and wished he could take the question back. Obviously, the man's death still hurt her.

'He was a volunteer for the local lifeboat,' she said quietly.

'Like Maddox?' he murmured.

She nodded. 'Dad was in charge of the crew. One morning they went out on a call to save a vessel in difficulty and…well, he never returned home. The weather turned rough and Dad fell over the side at the same time the ship they were rescuing turned over, sucking him under. A strange fluke, they called it. The way it occurred would probably never happen again. But on that day, with the sea as fierce as it was, unfortunately it did. Worse, he wasn't supposed to be on duty that week—

he was covering for a colleague who was off sick. If not for that he might still be alive.'

Logan reached out and touched the lone tear that had suddenly appeared at the corner of her right eye, hating to see the pain clouding her gaze as she silently relived the past. A cruel and significant event that had robbed her of a loved one. 'I'm sorry, Thurza.'

'Don't be. It's not often I talk about him to anyone. Rachel and her parents always become uncomfortable whenever I mention Dad. It's too painful for them to remember. The loss still haunts them. The sea is in my family's blood. They'd worked as fishermen and volunteers for the lifeboat for generations until Dad's death. It was their playground, if you like. My mum never understood that. She hated the sea. Resented its importance to Dad. Detested his loyalty to the crew. Considered the job dangerous and selfish, where loved ones are swallowed by the waves and lost for good. They argued a lot over Dad's need to volunteer. She never comprehended how he felt compelled to give back to the men and the association who'd saved his father's and his uncle's lives before him.'

'He sounds like a good man.'

Her smile this time was wobbly, but a

shimmer of light returned to clear the tearful mistiness from her eyes. 'He was. He always hoped I would join. When I was a little girl, I promised him that I would do my turn.'

'Did you want to?'

Thurza was silent for a moment, before declaring, 'I did, but I also wanted to do it for him. Especially after his death. It wasn't as if I'd ever be able to do anything else, was it? And even as a small child I knew how important it was to him.'

Logan shifted, resting his arm along the back of the seat. Sensing the importance of what Thurza was saying, he asked, 'So did you?'

She stared down into the half-filled mug resting on her lap and shook her head. 'No.'

'What stopped you?' he coaxed, sensing the reason behind Thurza not keeping her promise was important.

She hesitated before answering. 'My aunt encouraged me to train as a nurse first. Said it would be a good career to fall back on. She and my uncle took me in when I was seventeen and they hated the idea of me joining the lifeboat. They'd lost Dad and didn't want to lose another member of the family.' She hesitated again, then continued, 'The month before I found out I was pregnant I'd decided to send in my application. I'd enjoyed working at the hospital, but I missed home.'

Logan quickly put together the parts Thurza had left out. Her pregnancy had stopped her plan to follow her dream and keep her promise to her father. Guilt burnt like a rich, corrosive fluid throughout him. Another reason for her to dislike him. Without his meaning it to, his presence in her life, even for a short time, had generated so much change and disruption.

He searched his mind for some way to make it up to her. 'Perhaps you can volunteer now the twins are here?'

She shook her head, her expression becoming firm and stubborn. 'I've experienced the heartbreak of losing a parent to the sea. I won't do the same to the boys. They need me.'

'But if you want—'

'No, it's better to forget my promise,' she insisted, not letting him continue. 'The boys come first. My father would have understood. I'm happy with the way things are.'

But was she really happy? Logan wondered at the truth of her claim. Thurza might tell herself that she was happy, but her uncertainty and regret at not being able to follow her dream and keep her pledge to her father flickered deep in her eyes.

'And that's the only reason?' he asked gently. Intuition was telling him there was something else preventing her from keeping the promise. Something she'd failed or preferred not to mention.

She met his gaze for a second, and then looked away. 'Of course it is. What else would it be?'

He opened his mouth to reply, but the sound of whimpering coming through the baby monitor at Thurza's side stopped him. They both stared down at it.

'One of the boys must be awake,' she said distractedly. Picking up the monitor, she listened as the sound became a full cry.

He let go of her hand and offered, 'Would you like me to go and check? Only right I start doing my bit! If you're comfortable with me doing so.'

She smiled and nodded. 'Thank you.'

Logan stood and started across the small lawn to the cottage. At the back door, he glanced over his shoulder. Thurza still sat where he'd left her, eyes closed, face tilted to the sun. His heart flipped at the sight of her beauty, but he ignored it. Somehow he was going to make life easier for Thurza

Bow. Because he suspected that if he won her friendship it would be the best relationship he'd ever formed.

CHAPTER EIGHT

'MORNING, THURZA!'

The greeting from a teenage boy as she walked through the surgery's unusually quiet and empty waiting room the following morning surprised and concerned Thurza.

Smiling, she walked towards Mickey Russell, who was sitting with his grandmother. Thurza's eyes immediately spotted the small wet towel wrapped around the old lady's right arm.

'Good morning. What brings you to the surgery?'

Mickey pointed to his grandmother's covered arm, worry etching his young features. 'She's burnt herself again.'

Nannette Russell—or Nan, as everyone called her—fidgeted on the waiting room seat and sent Thurza a sheepish glance. Her straight white hair hung to her shoulders, held back from her face by a black hairband. Her pale freckled complexion appeared whiter than usual, and one of her wrinkled hands played with the edge of the towel.

Thurza took a seat beside her and gently asked, 'What's happened this time, Nan?'

'It's nothing, really,' the old lady insisted, sounding more apologetic than hurt and upset. 'I wasn't going to come down here and bother a doctor, but Mickey kept on until I agreed. He frets over me, you know.'

Thurza did know. This was their fourth visit in as many months. Nan's frequent accidents were becoming a concern, and something she intended to keep a close watch on. At fourteen years old, Mickey's role in his grandmother's life was slowly shifting from grandson to carer, and she was determined to make certain he received all the help possible to make things easier for them both.

'That's because he loves you,' Thurza said, spotting Logan strolling towards them. Dressed in black trousers and a plain dark blue shirt, he made Thurza's mouth water. 'Which doctor do you have an appointment with?'

'A Dr Fox,' Mickey answered. 'Gran's never seen him before. Is he new?'

Hearing the worry in the young boy's voice,

Thurza hurried to reassure him. 'Logan is our new locum, Mickey. And he's very good.'

'Mrs Russell?' Logan enquired, coming to a stop next to them. After a quick glance Thurza's way, he switched his attention back to his patient.

'Call me Nan,' the old woman said, getting to her feet. 'Locum, huh? Thought maybe Thurza had found herself a boyfriend.'

Thurza gasped, heat flooding her face and neck at the old lady's saucy remark. 'I already have two men in my life, Nan. They're enough for me.'

Logan chuckled, his interest on his patient and not Thurza. 'If you'd follow me, please?'

Thurza turned to Mickey as they walked away. 'Logan will deal with your gran's burn. Do you want to go with them or would you rather wait here?'

The boy gave Logan a sceptical once-over, before retaking his seat. 'Is it possible for *you* to go with her?'

Thurza turned to see Logan busy directing Nan through the set of glass double doors that led to the consultation rooms. Mentally running through the rest of her appointments, she nodded, eager to ease the boy's worry. 'My next patient isn't due to arrive for another fifteen minutes, so I can ask if Logan minds if I stay with your grandmother while he treats her.'

Mickey nodded and let out a relieved sigh. 'She's all I have, Thurza. I'd be in some children's home if it wasn't for her taking me in after my mother abandoned me to go off with that bloke. She fought the social workers, Mum *and* the courts to keep me with her. Making sure she's safe and well is the least I can do for her.'

With a reassuring nod, Thurza said, 'I know, Mickey. I promise Logan will treat her arm and have it sorted in no time. Don't worry.'

Hurrying after the other two, Thurza caught up with them just as they were about to enter the consultation room Logan was using. She hoped what she was going to ask didn't cause any offence. She knew some doctors would see the request as a possible slur on their ability and professionalism and dislike her asking. Hopefully Logan wasn't one of them.

Waiting until Nan had entered the room, Thurza pulled Logan to one side and asked, 'Would you mind if I join you while you see Nan? I promised her grandson I would. They've dealt with a lot of family problems over the last couple of years, and Mickey's become very protective of his grandmother.'

'Of course,' Logan said without concern. 'Perhaps he would prefer to join us?'

Thurza shook her head. 'He's happy to wait in Reception. He just asked if I would mind coming.'

Logan nodded and stood back so she could enter the room before following her inside. 'I don't mind your presence at all, Thurza. After all, who knows what else Nan may say to send your cheeks such an interesting shade of pink?'

After guiding Nan over to a chair, Logan took his own seat behind the large desk. He'd run through the old lady's notes before going to fetch her from the waiting room, and other than a recent run of burns she suffered no real health concerns. Surprising and pleasing for a woman of her age.

'Right, Nan. Let's take a look at your arm, shall we? I'm just going to examine the burn before deciding on the best treatment, okay?'

'Don't suppose you can prescribe a bottle of *you* to perk up my spirits?' Nan joked. 'I promise to enjoy a good daily dose.'

Logan smiled, but shook his head. 'I'm afraid not, Nan. Besides, I suspect the effect would soon wear off.'

Thurza moved behind Nan's chair and gently squeezed her bony shoulder.

Nan glanced up at her and enquired, 'Mickey sent you in, did he?'

Thurza laughed and nodded. 'He's a good boy to be concerned. This is your fourth burn.'

Logan carefully unwrapped the damp towel from around Nan's arm and inspected the burn, relieved to see no trace of butter or any other old wives' concoction her generation were apt to use to treat scalds and burns. No matter how many times people were advised not to do it, they still struggled to let go of the home-made cures learnt in their childhoods from their parents.

He studied the wound thoughtfully, relieved to see it was only a first-degree burn. Nothing too concerning. 'Painful. How did you do it?'

'Caught the saucepan while making Mickey's porridge. He likes a bowl when he comes in from doing his morning paper round. Warms his stomach lovely on the colder mornings at this time of the year.'

'Did you run it under cold water for ten minutes?' Thurza asked, moving from behind the chair to take a closer look. She crouched down in the small space between Logan and Nan.

Logan's fingers faltered and his pulse kicked up several paces at the unaccustomed sensation of Thurza's body so close to his own. The scent of floral-perfumed soap powder and warm feminine body crowded his senses, drying his throat as his body tingled from her proximity.

'Yes. I remembered you told me to do that when I burnt my elbow last month,' Nan answered.

Pulled from his distracted musings, Logan forced his attention back to the old lady and her burn. Thurza's body and its intoxicating scent were not his concern. His body just had to remember that.

As though to torment him further, Thurza rested a hand on Logan's shoulder to balance as she straightened. Her touch burned through the thin layer of his shirt to the suddenly responsive skin beneath.

'Were you wearing your glasses?' Thurza asked, dropping her hand and stepping back. She folded her arms and stared down at the old lady.

'Yes, but they need changing. I'm struggling to see out of them,' Nan admitted with a weary smile. 'It's no fun getting old.'

Thurza nodded. 'I think maybe you should make an appointment with the opticians this week. All of your accidents in these last few months have been caused because you're struggling to see and are misjudging distances.'

'Do you really think it will make a difference?' Nan frowned. 'Spectacles can cost an awful lot of money. I wouldn't want to spend out unnecessarily.'

Thurza smiled and reassured her. 'Yes, Nan, I do. At least have a test done and see what the opticians think. They'll be able to tell you if your glasses aren't strong enough.'

Logan stood, forcing Thurza to return to her original position behind Nan's chair. Grabbing medical supplies and a small white tray, he carried the items back and set them down on his desk.

'Well, it doesn't seem too bad,' he said. 'I think it will heal fine if left alone. I'll dress it with a bandage to keep it clean, but I'm pretty confident your body can deal with this without major interference from me.'

Nan lifted a hand to the delicate gold cross around her neck. 'Thank goodness. Mickey will be pleased. So how long are you going to be in town?'

Glancing at Thurza, he answered, 'I'm not sure what my plans are. I'm staying with my brother Maddox at the moment.'

How long he stayed would depend on how things progressed between Thurza and him. But for now he was happy to stay in Dorset.

Nan's mouth dropped open. 'You're Maddox's brother? Him with the farm up Lilly Lane?'

Logan nodded, not surprised that Nan knew his brother. So far nearly everyone who'd entered his consultation room over the last few days knew Maddox and Logan's connection to his brother. 'I'm afraid so.'

Nan's regard increased a level. Her eyes slowly wandering over him. 'You don't resemble each other much.'

Logan's smile wavered as he reached for a roll of bandaging. 'He carries my mother's looks and I my...my father's.'

Well, he guessed he did. Whoever his father was, he must resemble him genetically. He certainly didn't look like anyone else in his family.

Nan frowned and asked, 'Are you married?'

'No.'

Nan glanced at Thurza and raised her eyebrows. 'Not married, eh?'

Logan concentrated his efforts on dressing Nan's burn, hoping it would prevent her from asking any further personal questions.

Before she attempted to pull every last secret from him.

Once finished, he said, 'Keep the bandage clean and dry. The burn fortunately doesn't require a hospital visit and should heal completely in a few weeks. And I agree with Thurza over having your eyes tested, Nan. It won't hurt to make sure.'

Nan smiled at him. 'Well, if *you* think it's a good idea then I'll phone the opticians once I get home. Thank you, Logan.'

She held up her bandaged arm for Thurza to inspect. 'What do you think? Will Mickey be satisfied?'

Thurza smiled and nodded. 'Nice work, Doctor.'

Logan smiled. How polite and professional she sounded. As if they were two strangers working together for the first time. What would Nan say if she discovered that Thurza's children were his sons, too? He imagined the resulting gossip would certainly wake up this sleepy seaside town for several days.

'Thank you, Nurse Bow. I'm glad you approve.'

Thurza helped Nan up from her seat. 'Any problems—make another appointment. Don't leave it, hoping it will sort itself out.'

Nan glanced at Logan. 'She's bossy, but she's a very good nurse, you know.'

Logan grinned and nodded. 'I know. I think she's superb.'

Logan stretched out on the rug, elbow bent and head resting in his palm, full of joyous contentment. It started deep within him and filled every crevice, curve and gap until it reached his heart.

Happiness. True and unadulterated happiness.

It was an emotion he'd never truly experienced before. Not with his family or with his ex. And though the truth shamed, shocked and saddened him, it also gave him a real appreciation for the wonder of his new unexpected family.

His eyes never moved from the two babies lying on the light blue padded blanket beside him. Both were stretched out and fast asleep, wearing matching white dragon-printed pyjamas, snoring softly in the quietness of the cottage. His heart turned over with a rush of overwhelming love for these two boys, who in truth he hardly knew, but who now formed the centre of his life and whom he planned to get to know in every single way.

Thurza had accepted his offer to babysit

while she nipped to her cousin's house to retrieve a toy, leaving him in sole charge of their sons, whose every whim and requirement now concerned him. At first, he'd see-sawed from pleased to scared and then to excited. He'd never babysat anything before—let alone two small babies. But Thurza trusted him, even though he lacked any proper 'father training' or experience. And that show of complete belief, to be trusted by a woman who had every right to question and doubt him, meant everything to him.

Trained for nothing but medicine and doctoring, he now needed to learn how to do the biggest, most terrifying job of all. Being a parent. Someone for the twins to look up to and admire. Someone completely different from the two men who had claimed the role in his own life. One father who'd lied to him for years and the other one who'd walked away without a fight—turned his back on Logan without a care or regret.

To his thinking, if that man had borne any regrets during the preceding years then he would have tried to make contact with Logan—especially once he'd reached adulthood. The cold reality that he'd stayed away told Logan everything in regard to how the man felt.

Two selfish men, with no loyalty or affection for the innocent son stuck in the middle of the mess they and Logan's mother had jointly created. Had either of them cared about his feelings over the years? Had they wondered or lost sleep over the wrongs they'd done to him by not telling him the truth while they were alive?

He doubted Victor had. And his biological father had failed the moment he'd allowed his mother to keep Logan from him. Logan had loved his mother, but she'd had no right to make that decision. She'd robbed him of a relationship. Unlike Thurza, who'd tried to include him in their children's lives even though she'd received no reply to her letters and the evidence had made it appear as though he didn't care or want to know. She had tried repeatedly to build a link between him and their children.

During the last couple of days he and Thurza had formed a loose routine, spending time with the boys and each other when either of them wasn't working. Tonight, though, thanks to Thurza's invitation, issued before she'd hurried out of the house, he was spending the evening here.

He smiled, transfixed by the way each child's chest rose and fell with every breath. Small human miracles. Amazing. Just like their mother. She'd taken what fate had handed her and created a good life for her family. Not only was she good-looking and clever, but incredible and resourceful, too.

Letting out a contented sigh, he pillowed his head further into his arm. Yes, Thurza was wonderful. An impeccable mother to the boys. The kind of woman a man might picture keeping in his life long-term. The sort of woman a man could effortlessly fall in love with…

Logan blinked, then swallowed hard. Sitting up, he stared unseeingly at his surroundings while his thoughts raced back and forth. Dragging his fingers through his hair, he pondered that last notion.

Fall in love with Thurza? Now, that would be a bad idea. A really terrible one.

But…

Maybe it was the happiness budding inside his heart that had pushed his mind in that irrational and unwise direction. Sent him pondering over concepts involving commitment and love. But he didn't do love, and it was clear Thurza wasn't interested in him that way. Not once had she shown or indicated that she saw him as anything other than the twins' father.

The sound of the front door opening and closing drew his attention from his wild reflections. Getting to his feet, he met her at the lounge door.

'Hey,' he greeted her, shoving his hands into his jeans pockets. Mindful of the jumbled feelings still rolling through him, he tried to act relaxed. Did his thoughts show on his face for her to see? Noticeable like a guilty secret? 'Did you get Tyler's toy?'

Her bright smile set his heart into an aching backflip. She held up a small teddy bear in answer and waved it. 'Yeah. Any problems?'

'No, the boys haven't woken,' he said, noting the large glass jar circled with a purple ribbon and with a floral label in her other hand. 'That's a lot of honey.'

'Rachel keeps bees,' she said offhandedly. 'How about a cup of tea?'

'Can do,' he said, following her into the kitchen.

Desperate for a distraction to the thoughts in his head, he tried to concentrate on something else.

Thurza pointed to his laptop, though only

the back of the machine faced her. 'Busy working? Or playing computer games?'

'A little of both,' he admitted.

'There's a games console in the cupboard under the television, if you get bored any time,' she said. 'It's not new, but the games are pretty good.'

Surprised, he leaned against a kitchen cupboard and regarded her. How many more surprises did this woman have hidden? 'I never took you for a gamer.'

She shrugged and flicked on the kettle. 'I used to play on the nights I struggled to sleep, thanks to the twins wanting to play kick-about inside me. Of course, they may have just been kicking each other and I received the effects. I'm pretty good.'

Not bad himself, Logan asked, 'Any of those games for two players?'

'I think so. Fancy being slaughtered, do you?' she dared him with a grin.

He shook his head arrogantly. 'Won't happen—but if you're confident enough to try and prove differently, then how about we make something to eat and afterwards play a game or two? We can keep the volume low, so it doesn't disturb the boys.'

She laughed and retrieved two clean cups

from a cupboard. 'Trust me, they can sleep through any noise.'

He chuckled. 'I guess they must get it from me. How about it? You fancy taking me on?'

She grinned and met his gaze. Her eyes were sparkling with something more than just competitiveness. 'Oh, just try and stop me, Logan Fox.'

She meant it. Every single word.

Thurza sliced through thick bread that squashed down the moment the knife touched the crunchy outside crust. She'd take on the man and all he had to offer if he indicated that he wanted the same. The idea didn't repel her at all. She found Logan attractive, and the time they'd spent together had forced her to face the fact that, although she'd done her best to hide from the knowledge, she rather liked Logan Fox.

Actually, she more than liked him. She ached to talk to him about everything and nothing, to discover what he thought and believed. The way any woman would with a man she was attracted to.

Her cousin was annoyingly correct in her insistence that Thurza wasn't a one-night kind of woman. Many women happily shared brief moments of no real connection with a stranger, their target and desire being nothing more than a night of exciting and uncomplicated sex. No expectations. No ties. Just sex.

But not her. Her personality was far too emotionally open and needy for such a commitment-free physical interlude with another person. She sought a man who not only satisfied her physically while sharing her bed sheets, but also wished to develop a stable and long-term emotional relationship. Someone seriously into her and not afraid of commitment and family.

Yet with Logan all her beliefs had disappeared, and every day since they'd parted she'd wondered what had really caused her to sleep with him that night.

Yes, he was handsome, and at times funny. He also owned a serious side she found endearing, and he was the kind of man a woman could tell all her worries to and be sure he'd help her work through them…see her problems as theirs to sort, not just hers. A man able to view any woman he formed a relationship with as a partner and not a possession. Though his honesty over his reasons for getting engaged indicated that his skills for bonding with a woman still required work.

Would he act differently with someone

he loved? Someone special who owned his heart?

Thurza's parents' relationship had culminated in a battle of wills. They'd rarely tried to compromise. But she suspected that beneath the shine and polish of Dr Fox lay a thoughtful and compassionate male. His expression when he'd first met the twins melted her heart every time she recalled it. In that precious moment he'd looked like a man who'd finally found his true meaning in the world. As though a great internal mystery had finally been resolved for him and he adored the solution.

It had comforted her, and frankly she'd found it sexy. Behind the sheen of successful, capable doctor, the real Logan Fox appeared to be a decent, kind and considerate man. A good role model for the twins. A good person to have at her side in a positive capacity. A man she could care for.

But what did he think of her? Did he regret sleeping with her? Did he secretly wish another woman had given birth to his boys? Someone well off and more his kind? Not a small-town woman who worked at two jobs just to pay the bills and rarely spent money on anything new if she could find it cheaper second-hand?

She sprinkled grated cheese over the slices of bread and let out a short sigh. Thinking this way was dangerous and a waste of energy. They were co-parents and nothing more. Their relationship would stay completely non-sexual forever. No naughty carry-ons would occur once the twins were in bed. There would be no sneaky kisses when they sat next to each other. No touching each other's hands by accident. Fingers playing with hair would never happen. Nothing but conversation and friendship would take place. Simple and non-complicated. A loving, stable family circle without all the complex relationship stuff.

Never becoming something more than friends…

It was sensible and practical, if…rather boring.

Staring down at the half-made cheese on toast, she frowned. What if Logan decided to introduce a girlfriend or a new partner into their family? She closed her eyes and refused to deal with those thoughts. When exactly had she started to view them as a family unit, anyway?

She shook her head at her deliberations. No point jumping six steps forward. The future and its problems and concerns would soon arrive. Instead, she would finish their meal and then beat the smug devil at whatever game he'd chosen. For a couple of hours she would enjoy being surrounded by her sons and their father and try to not think about what her silly heart might quietly dream.

Because dreams rarely came true—especially when they were hers.

CHAPTER NINE

LOGAN LAUGHED AS Thurza swung Tyler through the air while attempting to sound like an aeroplane. One whose engine sounded on the verge of failing or catching fire.

Pushing Axel gently back and forth on a baby swing, he smiled at the giggles coming from his son. It was a sound Logan was learning to love each time he was fortunate enough to hear it. It filled him with joy and pride.

Despite it being early in the afternoon, the play park thirty minutes from Thurza's home was deserted except for them. Obviously the locals preferred to stay indoors rather than enjoy the wishy-washy sun of an autumn day.

However, Thurza had decided, after a morning working at the surgery, to wrap the boys up in their snowsuits, hats and mittens and take a long walk around the edges of town before stopping off at this neighbourhood park.

'Having fun?' Thurza asked, as she slid Tyler into the baby swing next to his brother and gave it a small shove that sent Tyler's arms flapping like a panicking baby bird.

'I am,' Logan said, meaning it.

Spending time with Thurza and the boys filled him with pleasure in a new and unfamiliar way. It wasn't just enjoyment from their company, but a peacefulness, too. A sense of being part of a group. *Their* group. Part of something important. He fitted in, instead of standing to one side waiting to be included—or, worse, being compelled to feel he had to earn his place.

Glancing around the park, he took in the five oak trees that lined one side. Their large, aged, weathered and gnarled trunks were wider in circumference than the width of both his arms linked together. An old-fashioned bandstand stood in pride of place close to a large expanse of grass, and it didn't take much to imagine a small brass band playing well-known tunes from the past during the warm weeks of summer, for the enjoyment of the listening public sprawled out on rugs or sitting on deckchairs while enjoying a picnic.

'This place is beautiful,' he said.

'It was first built in the Victorian period, after the land was donated to local residents by someone in the royal family,' Thurza informed him. 'A past queen mother, I think. I can recall playing on the original swings and slides as a child. The council removed them years ago, but you can still see clues of the park's Victorian beginnings if you look carefully at the railings and the gate at the entrance.'

They lifted the babies out of the swings and put them in their pushchair. Logan nodded towards a wooden bench and suggested, 'Shall we sit for a while?'

Thurza nodded, waiting while Logan brushed several dried leaves that had blown off the nearby trees from the slats.

'There you go.'

She smiled and sat down. 'Thank you, kind sir.'

Their eyes met once again, causing a fizz to spiral through Logan. His original plan of spending time with Thurza to stop his feelings growing for her wasn't working. If anything, they were becoming stronger, and he didn't know how to deal with them. It wasn't easy to continue to tell himself to ignore the feelings when something as simple as her smile set off sparks of awareness inside him.

To distract himself from the woman beside him, Logan forced his gaze to move over the scenery once again, taking in the muted orange, brown and green seasonal colours. A light wind danced over the park, shaking the odd cluster of dying leaves still vigilantly clinging to the otherwise bare branches of the oak trees, before their final drop to the ground below to rot and decay into a fresh layer of earth.

Logan had never imagined a small seaside town in Dorset could interest him. But his brother had developed a home and a living in this small town. Same as Thurza. She'd returned to a place she regarded as home. A safe location to raise their sons. It was a sentiment completely unfamiliar in Logan's own life. Yet over the last few weeks he'd started to view this place as more than just the town where his brother resided.

Did a home and roots in a place really bring happiness? Both Maddox and Thurza looked to have found contentment here. But what about him? If he settled in Dorset permanently would he discover the same? Or was true happiness shaped by the people a person surrounded themselves with?

If he stayed in this town with Thurza and the boys would he eventually feel the same way they did? See it as a shelter for his heart and solace for his spirit? Or would he eventually yearn for distant shores, unfamiliar green spaces and polluted city streets? Somewhere different and new? Would he come to resent the ties that rooted him here?

Thurza's affection for the town was deep. He couldn't imagine her being happy living somewhere else. She had relations, friends and patients here. Her memories of her father were here. Would she ever consider upping sticks and living somewhere unfamiliar? But perhaps she would love the idea of leaving this town for good. Would be open to the opportunity to move someplace new, where she could forget the past and refocus on a different future. Or would the ghosts of her previous family generations keep her here?

He suspected not keeping her promise to her father troubled her, despite her denials. If she applied to become a member of the lifeboat crew, even for a short time, would it soothe her conscience and lay to rest the ghost of her long-ago promise? Would it make her happy?

Yes, the job was dangerous, and every part of him struggled against warning her of the risks, but he refused to do that. Thurza more than anyone knew the dangers being a volunteer held. She'd faced and lived with the consequences of those dangers. Accidents happened, no matter how carefully people tried to make sure they didn't. But not fulfilling her dream and not keeping her word to her father was silently eating at her. He understood those emotions that called to a person and refused to leave them in peace. He'd heard similar ones once concerning medicine.

And if she did apply, and was offered a position, then his place belonged on land, caring for their sons so she could do the job free from worry or concerns surrounding her family. He'd be exactly where he wanted to be. So perhaps it wasn't this town that soothed a person, but this woman and the children whose appearance in his life fulfilled him.

Thurza nudged him with her leg. 'Tell me a secret, Logan. You know a little of my past—reveal something of yours.'

He let out a long heavy sigh, already knowing what he was going to confess, but struggling with how to say the words. 'A few months ago I discovered the man who raised me wasn't actually my biological father.'

Thurza gasped, whipping her head round to stare at him. 'What?'

His gaze moved to the twins, happily jabbering to each other in their pushchair. He couldn't imagine any reason or event big or painful enough to cause him to turn away from those boys. Or imagine carrying a vengeful desire to purposely hurt them in some cruel way.

'My mother indulged in an affair during their marriage and I am the result.'

'Oh, Logan,' Thurza said softly. 'That must be hard to take in.'

He continued as though she hadn't spoken, preferring to get it all out in one go. Ignoring it for months had felt a lot easier than confronting it did. But maybe it was time to pierce the festering wound and lance the venom from it.

'The information was only revealed after Victor—the man who raised me—had died and the funeral had taken place. And it was given to me through a formal solicitor's letter.'

'What?' Thurza gasped again. 'A letter? Not face to face?'

He shrugged, soothed by her indignation. 'Evidently a fake son doesn't deserve the respect of hearing the truth from the person who raised him.'

'Do I have this right?' she asked. 'The man who raised you as his own left you a letter telling you that you weren't his real son and didn't allow you to attend his funeral?'

'Yep.' Logan nodded. 'He instructed his solicitor to inform me of my mother's infidelity and my true parentage.'

Thurza shifted on the bench and lifted a hand to cup his cheek. Her bare fingers, though cool against his skin, gave him a measure of comfort. Her lack of self-consciousness when touching him eased a smidgeon of the anguish reliving it all brought.

'This man… Victor?' she asked, pausing to check she had the right name.

Logan nodded.

'Did he treat you as his son?'

'Yes,' Logan said. 'Not once can I recall him acting as though I wasn't. He always introduced me to his friends or business associates as his son.'

Thurza stroked his skin, her eyes troubled. 'Then why would he allow you to find out the truth in such a cruel way? Why didn't he tell you himself?'

He almost smiled at the outrage in her tone. 'I don't know the answer to that. I presume I was just a pawn in Victor Fox's long and manipulative game of revenge on my mother.'

She continued to rub her fingers against his cheek as though her touch could soothe away his hurt. He ached to move her hand and place it against his heart.

'Maddox believes that by not telling me,

my mother hoped to protect me from Victor's anger, but I'll never know for sure. The fact is they all lied, and it's not a pleasant feeling to realise not one person cared enough to tell me the truth. Their silence left me open to Victor's unexpected malice at the same time I was grieving his death.'

Thurza continued to caress his jaw. 'Why do people make relationships so complicated?' she asked. 'Why can't they just be nice?'

Logan chuckled, turning his head slightly to kiss the centre of her palm. The urge was too strong to resist and ignore. Suddenly he didn't want to talk about the mess of his family or contemplate the questions he'd asked himself many times over.

'Who knows? What I do know is how much I love your hair. It's very pretty and unusual. Especially the plaits.'

She smiled, lowering her hand before giving him a knowing look. 'Thanks—but don't think you can change the subject with corny compliments.'

Without another word Logan slipped his fingers into the thick blonde strands, pushing her hair tenderly away from her face. His gaze ran slowly over her suddenly flushed face. 'They're not corny. I mean every word.

You're incredibly beautiful, Thurza. Surely you realise?'

'And *you're* avoiding talking about your family,' she whispered, tilting her head back as his fingers started to stroke through her hair. Her lips tilted into a soft smile, indicating how much she enjoyed his touch.

'I'm trying to,' he admitted. 'But only because it's all very boring and you are far more interesting than my family's imperfections.'

She laughed. 'Smooth, Dr Fox. An obvious avoidance tactic, but smooth. I'm sure a lot of women would fall for such flattery and drop the subject—just as you'd like me to do.'

'But you're not going to, are you?' he queried, already knowing the answer. Reluctantly, he slowly removed his hands from her hair and sat back.

'Nah—not me,' she agreed. 'So, how do you really feel now you know the truth about your parents?'

He stretched out his legs and crossed them at the ankles, reluctant to search his feelings deeper, but aware that the woman beside him wasn't willing to cut him any slack. 'Why? Does it matter how I feel? It all happened a long time ago. Shouldn't I just forget it?'

She nudged his foot with her welly-covered one. 'Yes, of course it matters. The affair may have occurred years ago, but your knowledge of it is only recent. And I want to know because I'm nosy.'

He smirked, and for a long while pondered her question. For the last few months he'd purposely refused to confront any of it, only doing so once he was back in England and able to get answers. But even then he'd sidestepped exploring his own feelings too closely. Maybe by talking it out with Thurza he could make sense of it all and then forget it for good.

'I think the overriding emotion I feel is stupid.' Until he said the words he hadn't considered that aspect. But it was true. No matter how he looked at the evidence, it left him feeling a fool.

Thurza regarded him. 'Why?'

'How did I not realise?' he said. 'How did I not see that Victor and I shared not one physical resemblance? I mean most kids are a mixture of their parents, aren't they? So how did I not see—'

'Not always, they aren't,' Thurza interrupted, nodding to the twins still jabbering to each other. 'The boys are the image of you, Logan. There is nothing of me in them. Not yet, anyway. It might change as they grow older, or maybe parts of me will show in their personalities, but then again maybe not. Besides, I look nothing like my father.'

Logan rubbed his jaw. 'I always figured I took after a past relation—someone way back in the genealogy line. But I never really questioned it. Why would I? I was raised to believe Victor was my father. I never thought to question the truth of it. I wonder why I never once doubted it.'

'Why would you?' Thurza asked. 'You trusted your family to be honest with you. If they never gave you any cause to mistrust them, then why would you suspect differently?'

'I can't get rid of the feeling I should have picked up on something, though.'

'Were you close?' she asked. 'You and Victor?'

Logan leaned forward on the bench, linking his hands in the space between his knees. 'I thought so. We spent every holiday together. Right up until two years ago, just before his health started to fail. We went fishing for trout in Scotland. I honestly believed we were friends more than anything. Closer than most fathers and sons. He wasn't an easy man, but we made our relationship work. At least I thought we did. But he died and left instructions for me to be informed of the truth by letter and denied the chance to attend his funeral. I marvel at how good an actor he was. Either that or I'm nothing but a gullible fool.'

'He doesn't sound like a very nice man,' Thurza murmured, leaning her shoulder against his. 'And you're not a fool—or stupid. You're a good, decent man who trusted the people you thought were your family.'

Logan gave her a rueful look. 'Victor wasn't a terribly affectionate or loving human being. But he always treated me as though he cared. Now I see it was all a lie while he waited to get his final revenge on my mother and her memory.'

'I pity him, then,' Thurza said softly. 'Because if that was what he was doing all those years, then he didn't deserve you or your love. And *he* was the foolish and stupid one for not realising what a wonderful son he had. Blood connection does not make a father and son, Logan. Not always. Love does that. That can be stronger than a physical bond.'

'I never said I loved him,' he replied, suddenly uncomfortable.

'But you did and you still do. That's why it hurts so much. He should have treasured your relationship and your love. It's his loss. Because I know whoever you choose to love in your life will be very lucky and blessed.'

Logan placed his hand over hers where it lay on his lower arm and gently squeezed it. 'Complicated families, huh?'

She snorted and shot him an amused glance. 'Yes, they can be. Look at me and the promise I made to my father. You know, when we talked about him the other day it was the anniversary of his death, and not one person remembered. Not one. Thanks for listening to me.'

Logan slipped his arm around her and tugged her close to his side. 'Thanks for listening to me. Funny, but I feel better for it.'

She glanced away, but not quickly enough that he didn't catch the slight tremor of her lips. 'You feel foolish about not seeing the clues about your real heritage and your father, whereas I live with the burden of letting mine down.'

Logan pulled her closer into his embrace, desperate to ease some of her distress. He sighed. 'Thurza...'

'I want to believe he would understand why I didn't keep my promise and keep up the family tradition, but sometimes I wonder if he would be disappointed in me.'

Logan kissed her forehead. His own problems and disappointments were forgotten while he soaked in Thurza's own regrets and pain. 'I think your father would be proud of you. You're a wonderful person and a fabulous mother. Any man would be proud to father a child like you. I'm proud of you. It probably means nothing, but it's true. You amaze me.'

A tear rolled from the corner of her eye to trail down her cheek. A moment later a sniff followed it. 'But I feel as though I've let him down, Logan, and I hate it. It was the only thing he ever asked, and since his death I've put it off and tried to pretend it isn't important. But it's always there at the back of my mind. Constantly waiting to jump out and fill me with guilt.'

'The boys—'

'Are just a convenient excuse,' she said. 'The same way agreeing to train as a nurse was an excuse. My aunt wished it and I pretended to be against it for a while, but I wasn't really. A huge part of me was relieved to be able to delay keeping my promise. The truth is I'm scared to go out on the water in case the same thing happens to me as it did to my father. It's a feeling that has become stronger since I've had the boys. The worry is constantly there. That I'll go out one morning after kissing my children and never come home again. The same way my father did.

That my favourite jacket will hang on the peg in the hall for months before finally being thrown into a charity bag and lost for good. That my boys will sit on a lonely beach day after day, praying for my return, even though in their hearts they know that it will never happen. That they'll never hear my voice or my laughter again. That it will be an eternal loss that will never leave them, just as it has never left me.'

Logan's arm tightened around her, his heart aching at the grief in Thurza's voice. 'The job comes with danger. I'm sure your father would have understood your resistance and your reasons.'

'Doesn't nursing, too?' she countered. 'Every day medical staff are attacked by members of the public. Is the danger found out at sea and the danger in a medical centre or hospital so dissimilar?'

'Only you can decide that,' Logan said. 'But I think at some point you will need to make a decision and then find your peace with it. Because you shouldn't live the rest of your life fretting or feeling guilty. It's not right and it's certainly not fair.'

Thurza nodded, her attention drawn away by a squirming Axel, who'd grown bored sitting in his pushchair.

With a grateful smile, she left Logan's side and murmured, 'Our son calls.' Standing, she glanced down at him, a frown creasing her brow. 'I'm not sure I can make that decision yet, though.'

Logan clasped her hand and lightly kissed the back of it. 'You will. When your heart says it's time, you'll make it then.'

She nodded, her attention now fully on their son. Logan smiled as she bent down and kissed Axel's cheek.

Glancing up, she caught Logan's gaze and mouthed, *Thank you.*

His smile grew and he whispered back, 'My pleasure.'

Because it was. He'd do whatever he could to ease the burdens of this beautiful woman he was slowly coming to adore, and he wanted her to know that.

CHAPTER TEN

'Good morning, Alfred.' Thurza stepped into her patient's bedroom and smiled at the elderly gentleman propped up in bed. 'How are you feeling today?'

Alfred Blakeman sighed, his fingers tapping against the floral quilt and the knitted blanket that covered him. Signs of tiredness lined his face, but his brown eyes held their usual lively glimmer. 'I'm a bit cross today, I'm afraid.'

Thurza quickly checked through Alfred's medical notes and then asked, 'Any particular reason? Or did you just wake up feeling that way.'

With another sigh, Alfred glanced at the closed door. 'It's my daughter, Judy. She keeps wandering in every ten minutes and fussing. Good grief, anyone would think I was at risk of vanishing from this bed instead of dying in it.'

'Perhaps Judy just feels like spoiling you,' Thurza reasoned neutrally.

Walking closer to the bed, she gently picked up Alfred's wrist and checked his pulse. Unfortunately the gentleman's illness was terminal, but despite the doctor's original prognosis of less than six months, the old man appeared set on making sure he stayed around longer, just to prove them wrong.

'Yes, but sometimes a man needs a period of quiet time. A chance to have a wallow in peace. To think deep thoughts without interruption by mundane conversations about the weather, or if I'd like another cup of tea. I swear the girl is determined to drown me with beverages. How am I supposed to contemplate the mysteries of the next life if my daughter keeps coming in and disturbing me with questions concerning tea?'

Thurza chuckled and shook her head. Alfred's daughter was struggling with the prospect of losing her father. The two were very close and the only family they each had left.

People reacted to losing a loved one in various ways. Some, when faced with the reality of time running out, coped by pretending it wasn't real, or clinging to the hope of a different outcome. Others, like Judy, struggled against the confusion of mixed feelings. Although she hated to see her father so ill, she didn't want to lose him for good.

There was no right or wrong way to deal with loss. Grief and loss were as individual as the person enduring them.

'Would you like me to sort out your pillows so you can do your wallowing more comfortably?' Thurza asked with a smile. 'Might also help with this new habit you've developed of slouching to one side.'

'If you'd be so kind, my dear.' He gave her a conspiratorial glance, before whispering, 'Between you and I, sometimes when Judy does it I end up feeling like I've been shuffled and battered by a rugby player. She's always been a bit heavy-handed. Her mother was the same, bless her heart.'

'I'm sure Judy does her best,' Thurza said, plumping the pillows and gently helping the elderly gentleman to sit back. 'Any pain today?'

'Just a bit—but I took the medication the doctor prescribed. Nothing too bad. Tell me, how are those babies of yours?'

'They're as gorgeous as ever,' Thurza said with pride. 'Shall I take a look at the wound on your leg before we talk some more?'

'If you must—'

A knock on the door stopped their conversation and they both turned towards the unexpected interruption.

Logan, dressed in an expensive dark suit and holding a black leather doctor's case, pushed the door wider and stepped into the room. Musky aftershave with hints of tangy orange followed him in, tickling Thurza's nostrils with pleasing aromatic notes. Lately, she'd started to notice the same scent clinging to the boys' clothes, too. And she often found herself taking sneaky appreciative sniffs whenever Logan wasn't around to catch her.

But the man now entering the room wasn't the relaxed and teasing Logan she'd played computer games with, or the father who'd rocked their sons to sleep after playing at the park. This Logan Fox was the professional doctor she dealt with at the surgery. All charm, patience and capability.

Flashing a practised smile, he greeted their patient. 'Good morning, Mr Blakeman.'

Bright, confident and friendly, his smile was no doubt supposed to instil confidence in the person it was directed at. For Thurza it sent her heartbeat thudding and her stomach fluttering, as if she was a silly girl with an enormous crush.

'Logan... Dr Fox...' Thurza stammered, shooting their unexpected visitor a surprised glance. Did he want to speak to her, or was he here in a professional capacity? His smart clothes and his manner hinted at the second likelihood.

Logan sent her a reassuring glance, before turning to the man in the bed. 'I should introduce myself. I'm Dr Logan Fox. Dr Watts at the practice has asked me to pop in and let you know that for the next few weeks I'll be stepping in and taking over as your doctor. As I was passing, I thought I'd stop in and introduce myself.'

'Nice to meet you, Dr Fox,' Mr Blakeman said, waving Logan over to the empty chair next to the bed. 'Please call me Alfred. Though I don't expect I'll see that much of you. I suppose you know Thurza?'

This time Logan avoided looking in her direction and instead placed his bag on the chair. 'Yes, we share a couple of common interests.'

Thurza busily pulled on a pair of rubber gloves and folded back the bedding at the end of the bed to check Alfred's leg wound. Because of his illness, it was taking its time to heal.

Expertly removing the dressing, she spent several minutes checking the wound over, glad to have something to occupy her mind with Logan in the room. Lately, the sight of the man caused her thoughts to wander and her concentration to drift.

When she could dither no longer, she declared, 'Well, this appears to be healing nicely.'

Logan glanced over the folded bedding and also inspected the wound. With a nod, he turned his attention back to the patient. 'How are you feeling today, Alfred?'

'I was in a grump until Thurza arrived,' the old man told him. 'She always cheers me up. Known her since she was a small girl. Used to work with her father on the local lifeboat. Such a tragic day when we lost him. Real tragedy. Used to tell anyone listening how one day Thurza would become our first female member. Of course that was a long time ago. We've had a couple of female crew members since then. Ah, things change and life happens, I suppose...'

Thurza purposely closed her ears to the conversation and, after applying cream, redressed the wound with new coverings. Replacing the blanket and duvet over the old man's legs, she said brightly, 'I'll just get rid of these used dressings and have a quick chat with Judy.'

Leaving the room, she headed for the

kitchen, glad for a breather, away from Logan's presence and Alfred's talk about her father. She was not in the mood right now for either.

Opening up to each other at the park the other day, sharing their hurts, had changed something between them. The tangles she'd so determinedly tried to avoid were slowly knotting around them, taking them from casual acquaintances to friends with every deep secret they revealed to each other, leaving Thurza unsure of what she was feeling or where they were heading.

She'd weakened over Logan once before, but now every decision she made and every deed she committed affected two small boys. She refused to jeopardise their happiness and the calm life she'd worked so hard to build for them.

Logan Fox was a risk, wasn't he? And not one she was convinced she should take.

Logan stared at the door after Thurza closed it. The sound of her soft humming as she travelled through the house distracted him and lifted his mood. The woman, even on a chilly autumn day, evoked an impression of sunshine and joy in the atmosphere.

'She's a lovely woman,' Alfred Blakeman said, studying him carefully.

Uncomfortable with the old man's close attention, Logan refocused on the reason for his visit. With another smile, he suggested, 'How about I give you a quick check-over while I'm here?'

'I suppose you'd better,' Alfred conceded with a sigh. 'It is your job, after all.'

The old man waited for Logan to retrieve his stethoscope from his case and place it on his chest before saying, 'Her father was a good man. Thurza was his only child and he doted on her. They were always close.'

Logan nodded. 'Yes, she mentioned that.'

Alfred continued, 'Thurza was always a sensitive child, and I think his death hit her harder than most people realised. She was only a teenager. At a time in a young person's life when they require the steady hand of their parents, I always think. Her mother leaving and remarrying so soon didn't help.'

'It must have been tough for Thurza,' Logan murmured, only half listening as he concentrated on the sounds in the man's lungs.

'It was. Poor girl withdrew into herself for a long time. Stopped smiling as much as she used to. Of course, that's changed since she had her twin boys. Haven't seen her so happy and contented in years. Have you met them?'

Logan shifted and placed the stethoscope against Alfred's back, glad not to be hearing anything concerning or unanticipated. 'Yes, I have. They're great.'

'I believe Thurza regained what she'd lost when she had those children.'

Intrigued, Logan helped the gentleman sit back against the pillows. 'And what was that?' he asked.

'A family. It's what we all need and hope for, isn't it? If we're really honest with ourselves. We all want a family to fall back on. People around us who care. People who love you and support you. Thurza has her aunt and uncle and her cousin Rachel, of course. But it's not the same as your own close loved ones. I was raised in an orphanage until I was fifteen. Met my darling wife at the age of seventeen and grabbed hold of everything she offered. I may have been young, but I was no nincompoop. Man finds a good woman, he doesn't let her go.'

Logan turned away from the bed with Alfred's words echoing in his ears. *Family.* The very thing he'd recently believed he had, only to have it ripped away until Thurza came back into his life.

'Do you have a family, Logan?' Mr Blakeman asked. 'People dear to you?'

Automatically Logan opened his mouth to mention his brother, when a vision of Axel and Tyler floated into his consciousness. Yes, he did have a family. Those two small boys were his family. No matter what happened in the future, he was their father and always would be.

And Thurza? Was she part of that family? Could they make their situation work not just for a few months but for years? Could they build on their new relationship and continue to share raising their sons, or would time bring complications? What if Thurza met someone and wanted to get married? What would he do then? Where would he fit into that scenario? Would she be so keen to include him then?

The notion of some man living in the cottage with his sons disturbed him. Some faceless male he would end up having to share the boys and Thurza with. A man who would sleep at Thurza's side every night while he lived someplace else, alone and missing his family. And he would have to witness Thurza's love for the man each time he collected the twins for a weekend visit or day trip.

How would he face that when he was in love with her himself?

In love with Thurza?

Was that true?

Was he guilty of lying to himself for all this time?

Was the real reason he hadn't been able to forget her in all those months more than just infatuation?

Finally finding the courage to face the truth he'd spent so long avoiding, Logan searched his heart. He didn't understand how it had happened, and he had tried to pretend it hadn't, refusing to believe in love at first kiss. He had done his damnedest these last few weeks to prevent it from developing, while continually telling himself it wasn't appropriate or right.

The motive behind his desperation to leave England hadn't been just his broken engagement, but because at some point during that night he had fallen completely and wholly in love, and the strength of those unfamiliar feelings had terrified him. Their evening together hadn't just resulted in the boys. It had also been the night he'd secretly, unknowingly, handed the woman in his bed his whole defenceless heart.

Coming to Dorset and meeting her again,

spending time with her, had just confirmed what his scared heart had always known.

He was in love with Thurza Bow and he didn't know what to do.

Now that he'd acknowledged it, he couldn't deny it, or pretend it didn't matter. Because it did.

Remembering where he was, Logan pulled the stethoscope out of his ears and answered the old man's question. 'Yes, sir. I have two young sons.'

'How lovely. What are their ages?' Alfred asked.

Logan dropped the stethoscope into his bag and turned to continue with his examination. 'Just over ten months. They're twins.'

Alfred laughed and slapped the bedcovers. 'What a coincidence. Just like Thurza's.'

'Yes,' Logan said, turning as the woman in question stepped back into the room. 'Just like Thurza's.'

'Have you ever thought about dating?'

Thurza's heart turned over and she stared at Logan, who was wiping potato and mango splodges from Tyler's cheeks. They had just finished eating their evening meal and were in the process of clearing away.

'Er…no,' she said. 'I'm too busy.'

'I don't mean anything heavy,' he went on, giving Tyler's face one last wipe. 'I just wondered if you'd consider going out on the occasional date.'

Thurza spun around and plunged her hands into the bowl of hot washing-up water, glaring at the froth of bubbles as her mind tried to understand why Logan was asking. Why the sudden urge to discuss dating? Was he trying to suss out how she felt about the subject? Perhaps he had met some woman in town and this was his tactless way of letting her know? Hinting around the subject before slamming her with the news.

'Thurza?'

She shook her head and concentrated on her chore. Logan was a single man without any romantic ties. They weren't involved or partners. Who he saw and what he chose to do was none of her business.

Even thinking the words hurt. Struck at her heart like a brutal weapon intent on imposing agony. Who was this woman he was interested in? Did she know her? Was she suitable dating material? What if it was someone she didn't like? Oh, God, now she was starting to sound like her cousin. But how dared the man enter her life, insert himself into her daily routine, make her weaken and start to like him, only to sniff around some other woman within weeks. It was wrong, embarrassing—and plain hurtful.

'Honestly,' she said, slamming a china bowl down on to the draining board, 'I'd rather learn Italian than date.'

'Really?' Logan asked. 'Well, I can teach you, if you want.'

She glanced over her shoulder at him, not missing his pleased and rather smug grin. Her annoyance hiked up a level. 'You speak Italian?'

'Yes, my mother was Italian. I'll have you fluent in the language of love in no time. We'll need to practise. A lot.'

Confused, Thurza turned back to the sink. He had definitely sounded flirty when he'd said that last part. Or perhaps she was hearing what she hoped to hear.

Remembering his mention of dating, she asked, 'Are you trying to tell me that I'm boring and need to get out more?'

'"Boring" is a word that's impossible to link with you,' he assured her, coming to stand next to her. 'No, I'm simply curious over how you feel about dating.'

She frowned and thumped a plate down next to the bowl. Ignoring the shard of china that flicked off it and wrinkling her nose, she asked, 'Do you have someone in mind.'

'Yes.'

Thurza's heart dropped and she prepared herself not to be offended by whatever man he cited. No doubt it would be someone awful. Mouth dry, she waited for him to continue, already thinking up excuses to reject this mystery man.

'Me.'

She blinked down at the bowl of water, the degree of tension consuming her body reducing slightly. She glanced at him and repeated, 'You?'

'Yes.'

'You think we should date?' she asked, half relieved and half shocked by what he was suggesting. She reached for the tea towel on the worktop and dried her hands. 'You and me?'

He dropped the mango-stained cloth into the sink. 'Yes.'

'As in go out and spend grown-up time together? Meals, walks, lots of talking and occasional drinking?'

Logan laughed. 'Yes, all those and more.'

She glanced at the babies in their food-splattered high chairs. 'Aren't we a little advanced for that step?'

He shrugged and reached for the tea towel she still held. His large hands rested over hers, trapping them in the cotton folds. 'Does it matter if we manage our relationship in a different sequence to the norm? I think dating will be good for us. And that surely will benefit the boys.'

She silently considered him, not sure what to say. Part of her was tempted by the idea. She didn't want to be too scared to try a relationship, and she was sick with living in fear of something going wrong—but this was Logan, and whatever they did would involve their children, who would end up being hurt if it did all go wrong.

'You do?'

'I'd like to give it a go. Unless you think it's a terrible idea.'

'I'm not sure,' she answered, stalling. 'Let's be honest—if you hadn't come to visit your brother and found out about the boys, I'd never have heard from you again.'

'You know that's only because I never read the letters you sent. I would have been on your doorstep a long time ago otherwise.'

Which definitely meant that without the tie of their sons she would never have seen Logan again.

The sensual female inside her raged against

the idea that her main attraction was the twins. That Logan viewed her and the boys as a package, and her as a mother rather than a hot-blooded woman with sensual needs…a woman he couldn't live without.

Occasionally she allowed herself to fantasise over what it would be like to be closer to Logan, but the idea of changing their relationship worried her. Right now, they got on. Really well. What if that changed?

Logan shifted closer, as if he could hear her silent debate. 'Truth is, I haven't stopped thinking about you since we parted. You're in my thoughts all the time. Persistent, like a recurring dream. Taunting me with the memory of how good we were together. Night after night while I was in Malta I dreamt about you in the darkest hours and I swear I heard your voice whispering to me.'

Her green eyes wide, she joked, 'You may want to talk to a doctor about that.'

His eyes never shifted from hers as he continued to confess. 'Thurza, I desired more with you long before I learnt about the twins' existence. And since meeting you again, and finding out that I'm their father, I want you even more.'

'How can you be certain that it's not just the boys you want?' she asked. 'That your enjoyment of spending time with them isn't blurring your feelings towards me?'

One of his hands slipped under the material of the tea towel and found hers. 'Trust me, Thurza. I want you every bit as much. What you stir inside me is quite separate to what I feel about the boys. Don't ever doubt that.'

Licking her lips, Thurza stared into his face and faltered at the temptation he was offering with this talk of dating and desire. Should she agree and chance the possibility of heartache if it all went wrong?

Which it probably would. After all, he was Dr Logan Fox. He'd achieved his dream of being a doctor and he'd missed the birth of their sons because he'd been working abroad, helping others. She was a nurse, working two jobs and raising her children single-handed. She came from an ordinary family. She rarely saw her mother, because she couldn't forgive Thurza for staying in Dorset and not relocating to France with her and her new husband.

Would Logan be the same once he grew bored with the town and yearned for more exciting surroundings? Once the novelty of being a father and playing dad wore off, would he leave them? Or was she going to be brave, the way she craved to be, the way

Logan made her want to be, and grasp hold of all he proposed and do what her heart urged instead of letting her head take over? The same way she had on that night long ago when he'd asked her to go back to his flat and stay the night.

'Tell me what you want,' Logan coaxed. 'Tell me and I'll do it. Just don't ask me to leave. Because I won't. Even if you want nothing to do with me, or think us dating is a terrible idea, I refuse to leave the boys.'

'I'm not sure...' she started, uncertain how to explain her remaining reservations. The main one being not wanting to ruin the friendship they now shared.

Logan placed a hand to her face. 'I realise it's a lot to ask, but it's worth considering. All I'm asking for is that you think it over.'

She forced a smile and nodded. She could do that. She was an expert at thinking. Often, she thought so much she felt as though her brain would explode. She would sit down somewhere quiet and go through the pros and cons rationally.

'Okay. I will.'

Logan smiled and stepped away, leaving Thurza suddenly crushed and disappointed in herself. Why didn't she just say yes? Throw her arms around the man's neck and agree to the suggestion? Do a happy dance around the kitchen as a show of delight?

Because, as much as she wanted to be brave and say, *Yes, Logan. Let's date*, she wasn't confident that if it all went wrong she would be able to put all the pieces of herself back together again. Not for a second time, anyway.

CHAPTER ELEVEN

THURZA WASN'T SURE if it was the teddy bear lying in the centre of Logan's chest or the sight of the man stretched out on the floor in the narrow space between the two cots, fast asleep, that melted her heart into a slushy pool.

Standing just outside the twins' bedroom, she silently took in the sweet scene before her, not making a sound in case she woke any of the three occupants inside the room.

She and Logan had spent another pleasant evening together, but by the time the boys had gone to bed it had been late, and a storm had been raging outside, so Thurza had offered Logan the sofa to sleep on rather than get drenched walking home.

The dark shadows in the room suggested the time now must be around six o'clock in the morning. Too early to risk waking the boys after such a long and fitful night.

Normally they stuck to a good routine and she was loath to disrupt it. However, last night both boys had woken in the early hours. First Tyler, disturbed by the wind and rain hitting the bedroom window. He had refused to settle again, preferring to stay awake and be grumpy. Soon after, Axel had joined in the late-night gathering, rousing Logan from his sleep downstairs. At around four o'clock both babies, exhausted from their late-night get-together, had finally fallen back to sleep.

The last thing Thurza recalled was Logan guiding her back to her own room, with a promise to call her if the twins woke again.

A light snore from the male on the floor made Thurza smile. She tugged the scalloped edges of the patchwork throw she'd wrapped around her pyjama-covered body closer together. A nip clung to the air, searching out any gap or nook to fill with its iciness.

She frowned at the half-dressed man before her. Was he cold down there on the floor? Was a draught roaming over his body, ready to leave him stiff and aching to the bones when he eventually woke up?

Silently, she pushed away from the door frame and tiptoed over to where Logan slept. Careful not to bump the cots at her sides, she squeezed into the sliver of a gap and pulled the cover from around her shoulders. Leaning over Logan, she slowly and gently draped it over him.

Starting from his bare feet, moving up his unclothed legs and over his black boxers, she didn't stop until the patchwork cover swathed his T-shirt-clad torso. Letting go of the cover, she stared down at Logan, taking the opportunity to study him.

Oh, the man was utterly delectable. Truly gorgeous. His dark hair was ruffled and sticking up in places. Its untidiness added to his appeal. Despite what she liked to tell him, their night together had been far from disappointing. 'Hot' described it perfectly. Completely satisfying and utterly memorable. Her traitorous body hummed at the memory, but her sensible, cautious mind refused to dwell too long.

A second snore came from Logan, along with a throaty grunt. Thurza bit her lips to stop a giggle from escaping. Though she had to admit that even the man's snoring was attractive.

Unable to resist the urge, Thurza bent down and fiddled with the top of the blanket, gently tucking it closer around Logan's body. Her fingers itched to reach higher and touch the morning shadow that showed on his cheeks.

To skim the pad of her thumb over the rough-looking dark bristles just to experience how they felt.

If she lightly traced the outline of his mouth with her finger, would it feel warm and soft, like a plump cushion? If she leaned over and kissed it would he wake up? Or sleep through it the way he had on that morning months ago when she'd left his flat?

Warmth rushed over her at the thought, and shivers sprinted like silver flashes all over her body. She'd kissed him secretly back then to say goodbye. Now she wanted to kiss him and beg him to stay.

Forcing herself to back away from the temptation Logan's sleeping form provoked, she'd shuffled several inches away when Logan muttered, 'Thank you.'

His deep gravelly tone increased the quivers sparking along her skin. Sexy and sleepy. Delicious. Just like him.

'I'm sorry,' she whispered, inching near again. 'I didn't mean to wake you. I thought you might be cold.'

'Don't be sorry,' he growled. 'You can fuss over me any time you wish. I like it.'

She softened at his sleepy words. She suspected Logan hadn't experienced much fussing in his life. It saddened her to picture him as a child, growing up enjoying few hugs and cuddles. Those were the basics every child deserved from their parents.

'I'm not sure that's a good idea,' she murmured. 'You might get used to it.'

'I'll certainly try.'

She leaned forward, her hair falling around her face. 'Why are you sleeping here? Wouldn't the sofa downstairs be more comfortable?'

'I wanted to be close in case one of the boys woke again. I owe you where sleepless nights are concerned, remember?'

'I guess…' she said, touched that he was willing to let her rest so he could take his turn in caring for the twins. It was a luxury she wasn't used to.

'Besides,' he added, not opening his eyes, though he sent her a sleepy smile, 'no offence, but your sofa is a tad small for me, and after sleeping on Maddox's torturous one this floor is heaven. This is my first decent sleep since arriving in Dorset. My back will be grateful forever.'

'I'm glad,' she said.

Even with the barrier of the blanket between them she could feel the heat rising from his body, calling her own to recline into its comforting warmth and melt into his body.

'Go back to sleep,' she urged. 'It's still early.'

This time she shuffled completely away from the enticement of Logan. Before she gave in and took that forbidden step into the unknown. He might want to try dating, but did he really expect it to lead anywhere? Because Logan might admit to fancying her, but that didn't mean he wanted more. Didn't mean he wanted her and a future.

Despite what he said, if it wasn't for the boys she doubted he would still be in Dorset. He might claim to have thought about her constantly, but he'd stayed away and made no effort to look for her. If it hadn't been for his father dying they would never have met again.

So Logan Fox was a no-go zone. In fact, it would be best from now on to keep her hands off any part of his tantalising body.

'You can stay and share my blanket if you want,' Logan offered. 'I don't mind.'

Thurza licked her lips at the notion of resting into his body while the comforting weight of his arm encircled her back. While his naked muscular thighs pressed and moulded to her own softer clothed curves. She'd be wrapped around him like a human vine. Supported in his protective and wonderful embrace. Nice... Very nice to imagine. But far too dangerous to try.

Resisting every impulse silently beseeching her to push sensibility away and accept his wicked and tantalising offer, she continued to withdraw. She might long for Logan Fox, but she required serious commitment from a man. Would he be willing to offer her that or was dating all that was on offer?

'We don't have that sort of relationship,' she reminded him from the doorway.

Logan smiled and then sighed. 'A man can always hope for the impossible, though, can't he?'

Hope.

An innocent four-letter word, yet sometimes impossible. An impossible expectation or optimism for something a person longed for or aspired to.

Listening to her close her bedroom door, further down the hall, Logan silently acknowledged that it described exactly how he felt every time he spent time with Thurza. Nothing else counted but the woman in his company and his happiness at just being with her.

He rolled on to his side with another heavy sigh. That cliché about a person taking another person's breath away expressed totally how she left him. Breathless and aching—not just physically, but with a stronger, deeper and more spiritual hunger. As though their connection was more intense than anything he'd felt before.

This gorgeous woman lit him up and left him whole and contented. She gave him hope again. Real hope that wasn't stained with the blackness of deceptions and lies but held a simple, clean and amazing honesty.

She'd helped him to believe in the future once more. Despite their shaky start, he now regarded the upcoming days, weeks and years of raising their children with enthusiasm and optimism. Things he'd not felt in such a long time. For years all his life had entailed was work and further work. Now it centred around an incredible woman and two amazing boys.

After Victor's death and betrayal he'd imagined that the anger that had first consumed him would grow and expand, but instead a heavy and weighty numbness had settled in its place. Everything he'd trusted and thought true in his life had been wiped out without warning by a single letter. The good and bad memories, the infrequent family gatherings—all of it ruined and defiled by an old man who hadn't been able to find it in his heart to take some of the blame for his wife's infidelity. Who'd refused to bestow forgiveness upon a dead woman. His mother, whose memory Victor's hate and bitterness had tarnished forever for Logan.

He pulled the blanket surrounding him higher, sinking his nose into the soft, comforting fabric. Thurza's scent instantly filled his nostrils. The aroma was soothing to his serious reflections. He would never understand Victor's actions, but the pain wasn't as strong any more.

So, yes, he had hope. Only this time he wasn't going to allow anyone or anything to rob him of it. To steal away the thrilling expectancy building in his gut. Thurza was his and he was hers. And somehow he was going to convince her to give him a chance to prove it.

Because he loved the woman—he just didn't know how to tell her so.

Logan set Axel down in the sandpit and then placed Tyler on the grass. With two babies' needs to be concerned with, he had learnt to keep them both near, as they generally chose to do everything ten-month-olds shouldn't at precisely the same time.

Straightening, he glanced at the cottage and the left-hand upstairs window. Thurza still slept, but when the twins had woken he'd left his makeshift bed on the boys' bedroom floor and carried them downstairs for breakfast. That had consisted of two jars of pre-prepared food he'd found in a cupboard. He figured it wasn't often that they ate roast chicken and apple sauce for breakfast, but neither child had complained.

Checking that both twins played happily in their separate areas, Logan sat on the garden seat and flicked through his phone messages. Most related to work, except for one from Maddox, demanding an update on his whereabouts. Logan smiled at his brother's belated attempt at the caring older sibling role. It was years too late, but weirdly he appreciated the sentiment.

With another glance at the twins, he answered a text from a former work colleague asking if he was interested in a position overseas. Did he want to go abroad again? Would Thurza prefer him as a part-time father?

He glanced at the boys, his heart wrenching at the thought of leaving them. He didn't want to go anywhere. Every day the boys changed and learnt new things, and he didn't want to miss out on any of it. Yes, he could fly back to England regularly, but he'd still be a stranger who popped in and out of their lives.

And what about Thurza? They were slowly

finding level ground in their dealings with each other. Progressing from ex-lovers to something deeper than friends. They'd talked of dating. Thurza had agreed to consider it. If he left, they would need to repeat the process of getting closer every time he returned. No, he wanted to stay with Thurza and the boys permanently. How could he romance the woman if they were in different countries?

His thumb hovered over his reply before he finally pressed Send. The second it went, a new calmness settled through him. No regrets whispered in his ear. No indecision or doubts. One decision made and many more left to work through, but together he and Thurza would do it.

The sound of a strangled gasp jerked Logan from his musings. Flicking his gaze first to Axel and then to Tyler, he felt cold fear wash over him as he took in his small son's pale face and faintly blue lips.

Shooting off the seat, Logan swooped Tyler into his arms. His brain sprinted through a series of medical checks, before landing on the frightening conclusion that his boy was choking.

Flipping Tyler over to rest along his arm, so that his hand could support his head, Logan let his medical training take over, despite the petrified new parent side of him fighting to take control.

He slapped the heel of his hand down in the centre of Tyler's back, then repeated the action an extra four times. Turning Tyler over on to his back, Logan checked his son's mouth with his fingertips, flipping the baby back over when he failed to find any obstruction.

Silently counting, Logan slapped his hand down once again on his son's back. Biting back the cold fear attempting to push in, he forced his mind to focus. Repeating another set of four blows, Logan almost cheered when whatever had been blocking his son's windpipe was finally dislodged and flew out of his mouth.

Swinging Tyler upwards, Logan checked his mouth, breathing and colour, before hugging his small precious body to his chest. A mixture of fear, shock and relief sent him to his knees, still clutching his treasured baby to him.

'Thank God… You're okay…' Softly murmuring comforting words in his son's ear, he swallowed the jagged, smothering lump in his own throat, and gasped, 'It's okay, darling. It's okay, little man. Daddy's got you.'

'Logan?'

Glancing up, he found Thurza at his side. Dressed in her dressing gown, hair damp from a shower, she crouched beside him and wrapped her arms around them both. Her green eyes were full of concern.

'Is he all right? My God, when I stepped outside and saw you slap him...'

'He was choking...'

God, what must she have thought? Had she thought he was harming Tyler?

Thurza checked Tyler over, reassuring herself that he was okay and kissing him before stroking Logan's face with shaky fingers. 'I know you would never hurt him. I realised something was wrong by the way you held him.'

'We could have lost him,' Logan declared, the fearful words that had been crammed inside his head tumbling from his mouth as Thurza went to pick up Axel from the sandpit.

Why hadn't he watched Tyler better? Why had he allowed thoughts of work and Thurza to hold his attention instead of making certain his baby was safe? This was all his fault. *His.* What kind of parent was he that he couldn't keep his mind on his child and the possible dangers surrounding him? A terrible one—

that was what he was. One who had no right to look after his children or any children.

Shaking, he turned to Thurza. 'Dear God, he might have di—'

'Don't!' Thurza begged. 'Please, don't say it. You saved him. It's over. It's done.'

Done? It didn't feel done. The terror in his chest still compressed his heart and shook every part of his body. Tyler was crying right now in his arms because he'd neglected to keep him safe.

'It's my fault. If I'd concentrated on the boys and not my phone I would have seen him put it in his... He never would have... I—' He sucked in a wavering breath, shaking his head, barely able to speak as the cold reality of what might have happened poured through him once again. Because of his selfish neglect and distraction his child might have choked. 'God, if I'd never heard him gasp and looked up—'

'Stop it!' Thurza scolded. 'Things like this happen, Logan. We both know that.'

'Yes, but I should have—'

'No more,' she insisted. 'What was it, anyway? Did you see?'

He shook his head and clutched Tyler closer, needing the comforting reassurance of his small form close. Needing to hear his son's loud crying and feel the warm, regular temperature of his skin.

'I'm not sure. A stone?'

Thurza kissed Axel's head before searching the grass for the hateful item. Bending, she frowned. 'Ugh…gross, Tyler.'

Holding out her palm, she showed Logan a saliva-covered snail's shell.

'Maybe wait until you're older before you start trying foreign delicacies—hey, sweetheart?'

'A snail?' Logan stroked a hand over Tyler's head. 'He must have found it in the grass.'

Thurza inspected it more closely. 'Thankfully, it's just the shell. Mr Snail might have received a nasty shock and an unexpected wash if not.'

Tyler tried to seize the shell back, but Thurza closed her fingers over it and moved her hand out of grabbing distance. 'Let's get you a drink to wash your mouth out.'

'A snail…' Logan repeated, still feeling sick to his stomach as his heart rate slowly returned to its normal beat.

His son had tried to swallow a snail. A snail's shell could have destroyed their family and broken their lives forever. Robbed Axel of his brother and twin, leaving him feeling incomplete forever. Stolen from Thurza the child she adored and loved. Ripped his son away when Logan had only just found him.

'It could have shattered and cut his throat. What if—'

Thurza stroked his arm and pleaded, 'Don't do this. It's over. Those things did not happen. You stopped it from developing into something worse. You're a doctor. It's what you do. You're also a father, and I know you'll always protect the boys. Logan, your quick thinking saved our son. Let's just be thankful and count our blessings.'

'This time.'

He sighed, dark thoughts flooding in and replacing his initial distress. Pushing out all reason and sense. This time he had saved his child, but what if another incident happened, thanks to his lack of adequate care and concentration? What if next time the situation was worse and he didn't react quickly enough? What if he was too late or didn't see the danger…?

A new wave of nausea rose up and burnt his throat. He gasped. 'But what if next time—'

'You can't think like that,' she dismissed crossly. 'None of us can. We're parents, not psychics. We can protect our children as much as possible from hurt and harm, but we're also human, and occasionally things occur no matter how careful we are. Say a prayer of thanks and let it go. The same way you do when it's a patient you've saved.'

'But he's not a patient.' Logan shook his head, still too shaken to listen to her practical reasoning. Tilting his face to Tyler's, he inhaled his soothing baby scent. 'He's my child, Thurza. I should have done better.'

'You did what we all do, Logan. Your best. You're not to blame for the fact that our son has a curious mind and likes to put everything in his mouth.'

Logan slowly headed into the house, with Thurza and Axel following behind. She put Axel in the playpen and he handed Tyler over to her and stepped away from them both.

Everything Thurza had said made sense, but he couldn't get the sight of Tyler choking out of his head…his blue lips and the sound of his gasping breath as he'd struggled for life. Although in real time it had played out in only seconds, in his head it ran at a slower speed, over and over again, his memory seeing it all on gut-wrenching repeat.

Stomach rolling again, and unable to deal with logic thanks to the swirl of emotions still seizing every part of him, Logan continued to back away. A few seconds' delay and the outcome would have been different. Tragedy had been just seconds away from occurring. And if it had Thurza wouldn't be thanking him. She would be shouting at him for his negligence. Hating him for failing their son. And she would be right.

It was all his fault. No one else's. He wasn't fit to be a father. No more than his own fathers had been. Wasn't it better to leave now, before his sons were seriously hurt? Before he ruined their lives and the safety Thurza had worked so hard to give them? They deserved better than a careless father.

Shaking his head, he stammered, 'I—I need to leave.'

'Please, Logan, don't,' Thurza begged. 'Please, stay and—'

He didn't trust himself around this astonishing woman and their beloved two boys any longer. 'I'm sorry, but I need to go. I'm sorry…'

He stumbled away and left the house, shutting out the cries of each boy and Thurza's continued appeals to stay. He needed to think…to process everything. One second was all it took. One stupid moment was all it required to lose a child forever. Was this a sign that he wasn't cut out to be a parent? One he shouldn't ignore? Would his new family be safer without him in their lives?

* * *

Thurza pushed the double pushchair along the lane towards the beach. It was the one place she had yet to search. If she didn't find Logan soon she would have to give up and return home. The boys were due a feed and the weather had turned cold and misty.

Rolling off the pavement and on to the promenade, she scanned the area for the sight of a familiar male. The man who had left her house several hours ago, upset and full of needless remorse and guilt.

In the distance, despite the mist coming in off the sea, Thurza could just make out the end of the Victorian pier on the east side of the beach. At this time of year the council closed it to the public to save money, so it stood abandoned, with neither visitors nor local fishermen.

Other than seagulls and a lone weathered wooden boat, long abandoned by its owner, nothing littered this stretch of shore.

Her gaze shifted to the sea and then back to the pebbled beach. Having already checked Maddox's farm and the doctors' surgery, on the off-chance that Logan might have gone to either, she found her list of possible places to search shrinking. The man was more elusive than a ghost during daylight hours. She understood his need to be alone after the incident with Tyler and the snail, but the way Logan had left, and the state he'd been in, worried her.

She completely understood his reaction. Their jobs involved caring for strangers, but when your own loved one needed care the balance tilted into uncomfortable and unfamiliar territory. Just because they were medically trained, it didn't mean that when faced with a critical situation involving the life of their own child it didn't reduce them to feeling the same terrifying alarm any other parent would experience.

But the expert way Logan had dislodged the snail shell and then comforted their frightened, crying son sent goosebumps of pride and fear all over Thurza each time she recalled it. The moment he'd hugged Tyler with relief, before the self-recrimination had taken hold, would stay with her forever. That display of love for his child had been stronger than any words or deed. That act of love had given her the courage to make a decision of her own that would affect all their futures.

The man believed he'd failed their child, whereas she viewed him as a hero. *Their* hero. Hers and the boys'.

She hated the idea of Logan beating himself up over what happened. She ached to comfort him the same way he had her at the park. He hadn't criticised her or pushed her to make a decision over the promise to her father. Hadn't called her a coward when she'd admitted her own fears. No, he'd held her and let her know he understood. And now she wanted… Well, she wanted to ease his distress and help him in every possible way.

She'd loved their playful conversation that morning. His dubious offer to share the patchwork throw and snuggle into him had lifted her heart like a butterfly hovering in the air, leaving her deliberating over whether taking a chance on a real relationship with Logan would be worth the gamble.

But deep down she already knew the answer. A relationship required more than just sex to grow strong and solid. It required time, friendship, common interests and…love.

Love.

Yes, she'd dilly-dallied over accepting how she really felt. But after the incident with the snail's shell she'd finally opened her heart and searched its depths and accepted the truth in all its glorious colours. The truth that made her yearn to shout with joy.

She loved Logan. Not because of the boys, but because of him. Everything felt right whenever he was close. She was ready to accept his offer to date and to leave the future to unfold itself without worrying over how it would end.

But did Logan still want her?

Oh, he'd accepted his children, and his affection and love for them was obvious, but what about her? Did he still want them to date? Or had this morning's events scared him off? Had his concern over his so-called inability to protect his children changed his mind? Did he want them to be a family? A real one? Did he want her?

Perhaps he intended to return to work overseas and become a now-and-then father after all. One who sent postcards and letters and visited on holidays and birthdays. The 'guilt days', as she tended to think of them. Like her own mother after she'd married her second husband. Dutiful visits carried out mainly to ease her conscience.

Would the episode with the snail send Logan back to Malta? Back to his life as a single man, without responsibilities to a family he had never intended to form?

Thurza's footsteps slowed as she recognised the male figure alone on a bench several feet away. *Thank goodness.* Pushing the buggy towards Logan, she didn't stop until she reached the other end of the bench. Parking the boys between them, she took a seat and stared out at the sea. Though not much of it was visible thanks to the mist.

'Thurza…' Logan began, but she shook her head to stop him. He could talk after she'd said what she'd come here to say.

'I'd really appreciate it if you'd let me speak first,' she said, still not looking his way, finding it easier to speak without facing him. If he did plan to leave, she didn't want to see it on his face—not before she'd said her words.

He shifted on the bench but stayed silent. The lapping of the waves against the pebbled shore was the only sound in the air.

'I would have loved having you at my side during my pregnancy. Even just as a co-parent and nothing else. I felt so alone and uncertain about how I was going to cope with everything. From the birth, to caring for the boys and earning enough money to keep us.'

'I know. I wish I had been here,' he murmured.

She nodded and continued, 'When I first took the twins home I was terrified. A nurse, with all my training and knowledge, frightened by the reality that I was solely in charge of these two very small and vulnerable babies. Their little bodies seemed so small and delicate… And then they liked to wake at the same time and be fed at the same time. They also cried together, and I swear they did it just to see who could scream the loudest. Long, tiresome nights…but I dealt with every single one and managed to get through each day. Honestly, I'm not sure how. Rachel stepped in so I could grab extra sleep. She's so good to me, and she helps with the twins when I work, but honestly it's not the same as being able to turn to someone special…someone close who is there in the middle of the night and prepared to jump in when I need an extra hand or a moment just to take a breath. Like you did last night, Logan.'

She sensed him shift again, but he didn't speak. He was giving her the time she'd asked for to say what she needed to.

'Over the last few weeks,' she continued, 'you've helped me, and I am grateful. But it's also made me realise how much I like having you around. I enjoy your company, Logan. Very much.'

'I like being with you, too,' he admitted.

Finally, she turned to him, taking in the stress etched across his features. Licking the mist from her lips, she said, 'What happened earlier was just one of those things. It's life. It's being a parent. You're a human being, not a superhero. Though to me you come pretty close. But you have to stop expecting to be a perfect parent, because they don't exist. Every single parent is just doing the best they can. Babies are quick, and curious, and they will do things that scare us. That will continue as they get older, and all we can do is stand to one side and try to stop the situation from becoming scary while allowing our children to learn how to be independent.'

Logan sighed heavily. 'I know you're right. It's just…'

She slid closer to him, smiling as she reached for his cold hand, hopeful that he wasn't going to leave. *Please, don't let him leave.*

Wrapping her fingers around his chilled skin, she said, 'I know. It's hard to admit that we can't always be in control of life. It's similar to how I feel about volunteering for the lifeboat. It's the fear of the unknown. And instead of facing it I've permitted it to become a huge blot in my life, to the point where it has grown and grown until it's controlled me. But you'll be happy to hear I've made a decision.'

'And…?'

Hesitantly, she took an envelope from her coat pocket and showed him the address written on the front. 'I've filled out an application form. All I have to do is post it.'

Logan squeezed her hand, the action both supportive and reassuring. She'd decided it was time to stop faffing around and letting fear dictate her life. She would send the form. And if she made it through the training and was offered a position on the team then it would be for *her*. Not because of a promise to her father, and not because of guilt. But because she was Thurza Bow and she wanted to do her turn for her family. Because she refused to let fear dictate her actions and her life.

She looked up at Logan and said, 'And if they accept me...'

'Then you'll take it,' he said instantly. 'Worry less about what you can't control. You need to do this. Until you do, I don't think you'll ever be able to let the past rest. Grieving is natural, but yours is mingled with remorse, and I'm certain your father wouldn't have wanted that.'

'What if one day I go out into a storm and the rescue goes wrong, the way it did with my dad, and I never come home again. What about the twins?' She glanced at the man beside her. *What about you? Will your heart grieve for me? Will you step in and raise our babies alone?*

'Like I said—stop fretting. It's useless to

try and second-guess what tomorrow has planned. I'm here for the boys forever—you know that, don't you?'

Deep down, she did—though she still couldn't ignore that he'd only mentioned the twins and not her. 'Yes.'

'I think the question is whether you're ready to send that form. Ask yourself what you want, Thurza. Deep in your heart, what do *you* want? Yes, things may go wrong, but we can say that about all situations in life. A person can start a normal day that within a few hours can change them forever. As a nurse, you're aware of that as much as I am.' He gave a wry laugh and shook his head. 'Tyler's antics this morning demonstrated that perfectly, didn't they?'

'It was the prod I needed to make my decision.' She stared at him, searching his face, and asked, 'Are you all right now?'

He nodded. 'Yeah, sitting here has helped to put everything into perspective. I'm sorry if I upset you by rushing off the way I did.'

Reaching into her pocket again, she dismissed his concern, relieved that he wasn't planning on leaving them. Silently, she handed him a scrap of paper and waited while he unfolded it and read the telephone number written across it.

'What's this?' he asked, confused.

'It's the number for the local registrar's office. I thought we could ring them and enquire about adding your name to the boys' birth certificates.'

Tears entered Logan's eyes and he glanced at the number on the piece of paper again. With a cough, he asked, 'You're happy to do that? I mean, it's what you want?'

She smiled and nodded. 'It is. It's only right that your name is on the documents along with mine. We're both Tyler and Axel's parents, after all.'

'We are.'

She met his gaze again, sucking in a quick breath at the tenderness and happiness shining in the blue depths. The anxiety and guilt of that morning were nothing but an ugly memory.

'Can I kiss you, Thurza?' Logan asked seriously.

Her eyes widened at the question. Her heart still fluttering at the sight of the emotions in his gaze, she tilted her head to one side. 'Are you propositioning me on the promenade, Dr Fox?'

A rakish grin tilted his mouth. 'Yes, I think I am.'

'Then you'd best get on with it. I need to get going and send off my application.'

He laughed, and on the misty, deserted beach, in front of a lone squawking seagull and not much else, he kissed her.

And then, to Thurza's absolute delight, he kissed her some more.

CHAPTER TWELVE

SEVENTEEN TIMES HE'D tried to talk to her. Seventeen. He knew the exact number because he'd counted each and every attempt. Logan gripped his bottle of beer and watched the woman people insisted on speaking to lift yet another large pumpkin off the ground and into a mud-coated wheelbarrow.

In a fit of genius, Maddox had invited all his friends and neighbours over to the farm to help gather in his vast pumpkin and squash crop. In return he'd handed out mugs of tomato soup, foil-wrapped cheese-sprinkled baked potatoes, cooked in his outdoor brick oven, and sparkler fireworks.

And it seemed as though every person who'd turned up to help wanted to speak to Thurza at exactly the same time Logan did. Every single one.

Taking a swig from the bottle, he sighed as yet another person sought out the woman who distorted every sane thought and emotion in his head. Thurza, whose letters, written and posted long ago, he'd finally read after he'd asked his cleaner to pack them all into an envelope and forward them to him.

The letters had broken his heart on reading them, and left him once again wishing the past could be rewound.

Those words on floral lined paper had started off apologetic and embarrassed in tone, as she'd politely informed him that she was pregnant with his child. Later the letters had become chattier, as she'd recounted the various stages of her pregnancy and her shock and excitement at discovering she was carrying twins. In one letter she'd even included the time and place of a scan, in case he wanted to join her at the appointment.

Unsurprisingly, the last few letters had turned cold and crisp, matter-of-fact in manner, as she'd accepted his lack of interest and promised not to bother him again. Her disappointment in him pulsed from every word and pen stroke on the page.

But the letters, although despondent, had given him faith in their future. And renewed his hope.

With a heavy sigh, he took another gulp

of his beer, softly growling when yet another person called out to Thurza.

Perhaps if he dragged her into the farmhouse and up to the bathroom he could lock the door and barricade them inside by stacking towels and the large clothes basket against it. Then he might finally get the opportunity to say the words that rambled through his mind. The words keeping him awake at night and thoughtful all day. Words he was half terrified to say out loud and half dreaded her reaction to. But he knew deep inside that it was time for them to be said.

Since their heart-to-heart on the promenade he'd practised, rehearsed and edited the declaration bubbling and vibrating in his heart. Shifting and sorting his thoughts and feelings into a comprehensive pronouncement until he knew it by memory. With one chance of getting this right, and hopefully getting the result he desired, the pressure increased with each passing day he kept his thoughts to himself.

'But what if she says no?' he muttered softly. What would he do then to convince her that they should be a family in the true sense? That they belonged together.

'Why would she?' Maddox demanded at his side.

Logan jumped, not realising his brother stood nearby. His already stretched nerves increased with his sibling's company. 'How long have you been there?'

'Long enough for my stomach to turn at the soppy way you're staring at the woman,' Maddox complained. 'Look, you're perfect together. Like bread and butter. Cheese and chocolate. Just stop with the mooning expressions, will you?'

'But does she feel the same way?' Logan muttered.

Maddox shrugged and tugged off his worn leather gardening gloves. 'Too much deep thinking for me, bro. But she must do, seeing as she gave birth to your children. The only way to get an answer to that question is to ask. Now, stop staring at Thurza like a lovesick moron—you're scaring the children and it's embarrassing, watching you pining. Do I need to drag you over to her like an embarrassed teenager with his first serious case of the hots?'

Logan huffed and shook his head as yet another person stopped to speak to Thurza. 'There's no point. I can't get a chance to talk to her alone with everyone else determined to beat me to it.'

'Well, in that case,' Maddox said, placing

his arm around Logan's shoulders and giving him a hard squeeze, 'let me make a suggestion—'

'No!' Whatever his brother was going to suggest he'd ignore. He could mess up his life without Maddox's help.

Maddox squeezed him harder. 'Trust me, will you?'

'Why should I?' Logan asked, already certain that whatever Maddox proposed to do would be a disaster. Relationship advice and his brother did not go together.

Maddox grinned. The light of mischief in his eyes was almost frightening. 'Because I'm your big brother and I always triumph with the ladies.'

Logan snorted. 'You're lying.'

Maddox chuckled. 'Like I said…just trust me.'

Logan wasn't sure he could, but right at that minute he was a desperate man.

'Sorry to interrupt, but I need you.'

Logan smiled politely at the older lady talking to Thurza, before slipping an arm around the woman he loved and guiding her away from the squash-gathering throng and over to a dark corner of the pumpkin field.

'Is something wrong with the boys?' Thurza asked, concerned. 'I thought Rachel—'

'The boys are fine,' Logan soothed. 'But I am not.'

'Is Rachel still glaring at you?' Thurza asked, concerned. 'Because if she is I'll talk to h—'

Logan laughed. 'No, she has turned her attention to finding ways to keep the boys from Maddox. Apparently, the idea of having to share them with an uncle is too much for her to absorb.'

'So why do you need me?' Thurza quizzed.

Logan drew in a deep breath, grasping the opportunity to finally talk to Thurza. But saying the words now he had her attention wasn't going to be easy. 'It's my chest.'

'You're feeling ill?' she asked with a concerned frown. 'Why didn't you say so? Doctors make the worst patients.'

'No, I mean it's my heart,' Logan stated, tugging her towards a bulldozer.

Its large bucket was raised a foot off the ground, and several thick padded cushions she recognised from the garden chairs scattered around the property rested inside, forming a makeshift seat.

'Your heart?' Thurza repeated.

'Yes,' Logan said, pulling her down on to the cushions. 'Let me show you.'

'What are you doing?' she asked, as the bulldozer's engine suddenly roared to life.

A second later Logan's arms slid around her waist and he yelled, 'Take her up!'

'Logan!' Thurza grabbed hold of his jumper and clung to him as the bulldozer's bucket slowly started to rise into the air.

He grinned at her startled expression and leaned back, happy to protect her. 'I'll stop you from falling. Rest into me and I'll keep you safe.'

'Why is this thing moving?' she demanded, closing her eyes when the top of a nearby tree came into view. 'I'm not sure I like it.'

'Imagine you're on a fairground ride. Don't worry—we're not going anywhere. I would simply like to talk to you without everyone interrupting us.'

Concern wrinkled her brow. 'You want to talk?'

'Yes,' he said, trying to recall exactly what he wanted to say. His stupid brain had frozen and stolen the words away. Instead, he said, 'Stop it.'

Confused, she stared at him. 'What? I'm waiting for you to speak. You're the one who wants to talk.'

'I know, but you staring at me with those big green eyes just makes me want to kiss you.'

She smiled and glanced away. 'You're a man with a weakness for kisses, aren't you?'

'Only yours,' he said. 'They're perfect and sweet-tasting.'

'Thank you,' she said, glancing back at him. 'Now, confess—what's wrong with your heart?'

'You,' he stated.

'Me?' she repeated, raising both her eyebrows in surprise.

'And the boys,' he added, not forgetting the other two most important people in his life. The sons who for a while he hadn't known, but who now filled his days.

'The boys?' she repeated slowly. 'And me?'

He nodded. 'Me, too.'

She laughed and shook her head. 'All four of us, then?'

'Yes,' he said, then sighed and dropped his head on to her shoulder, breathing deeply as his mind struggled to find the right words. The ones he'd so carefully composed. 'I'm messing this up, aren't I?'

She giggled. 'I'm not sure what "this" is, so I can't say. I *am* confused, though.'

He lifted his head and stared into her eyes.

'All right, here goes. Thurza Bow, you are an amazing woman and a fantastic mother. If I searched all over the world I'd never find anyone like you. You are uniquely magnificent.'

She waited for him to continue. The lowering darkness and the shadows around them made the moment extra intimate. Up here, away from the people on the ground, it was just the two of them.

'You're delightful,' he said.

'Like my kisses?' she teased shyly.

'Precisely.' He nodded. 'And I think… No… I *know* that I love…'

'Love?' she whispered.

He took the surprise on her face as a good omen and pushed on. 'I love having you in my life. You and the boys are a gift, and I want to ask…'

'Yes?'

He reached out for her hand and rested it against his chest. The heat from her palm radiated through his green jumper to warm his heart. An organ that had always functioned well enough, but until he'd met Thurza hadn't known what true passion and affection felt like.

'Can you feel my heart, beating like a runner's during a race?'

She nodded, spreading her fingers out where they lay on his chest.

'This is what you do to me, Thurza. You make me nervous and excited and desperate to be with you. I've never experienced these emotions before. With you I don't think or plan. I just feel. You make me want a future—one with you and the boys. One where we're a real family. The four of us and any other children who may or may not arrive. Thurza, I love you, and I want to make it official. I want to be in your life from this day until my last. I yearn to sit with you on your garden seat and watch our children grow. I want to watch you smile first thing in the morning and to kiss your sweet lips late at night. I want to sing to you on your birthday and present you with ridiculous anniversary gifts that make no sense to anyone but us. I want to be your—'

'I want to hold your hand the first day our boys go to school and cry on your shoulder as they wave goodbye,' Thurza said, taking over from him. 'To peel mountains of vegetables with you on Christmas morning and then collapse on the sofa together and sleep the afternoon away. To cry at your side when the days are tough and laugh on happier ones. But mostly I want to be your—'

'Husband.'

'Wife.' She finished a second after him.

'How's it going up there? Do you want to come down yet?'

Logan grimaced at his brother's untimely interruption. Without pause, he shouted, 'No! Go away!'

'We're getting married!' Thurza called out laughingly, desperate to yell the news to the world.

He loved her. He'd said the words and her heart knew he meant them. Just as she did. No more worrying over whether to take a chance on a relationship. They were already in one. The day he had demanded to know if her sons were his, their destiny had been set.

'Are you sure you don't want me to lower the bucket?' Maddox yelled up.

'No!' she answered. 'There's things we still need to discuss.'

Logan's happy expression dimmed at her comment, and a worried frown creased his forehead. 'Such as…?'

Shuffling closer, she gently grabbed the sides of his face and said, 'I think we should practise our kisses. It requires a lot of work to maintain such an important skill.'

Eyes shining with happiness, he grinned. 'I agree.'

Moving nearer, she whispered, 'Kiss me, Logan Fox. Kiss me until we hit the stars above us and bang our heads on the moon. Let's go for a whirl around the Milky Way, and Venus, too.'

'Why not?' he agreed. 'I already feel like I'm in the heavens whenever I'm with you.'

Without another word, he did as she'd asked, happy to take orders if it meant kissing this beautiful, sweet woman, because he loved her. Truly and completely. Forever.

And this time he wasn't running away because he was scared of the feelings she awakened inside him. He intended to stay and enjoy them all.

EPILOGUE

THURZA LET OUT a relieved breath as they finally located the surfer, desperately clinging to his surfboard in the grim swirling sea.
After bumping over the waves for ten minutes without any sign of the teenager, she'd
started to worry they were too late.

Wiping the rain out of her eyes, she pushed
back the strands of hair stuck to her cheeks
and leaned over the side as her boss carefully
manoeuvred the lifeboat closer to the surfer.

'It's okay!' she called out to the exhausted
boy, still clutching his board. His fingers and
knuckles were white with fear and the cold.
'We've got you now.'

'I'm so sorry…' the teenager gasped out.
Seawater splashed into his face as he struggled to hold on.

Thurza leaned forward and slipped her arm
under the teenager's armpit. With the help of
a colleague, she pulled the surfer out of the

water and into the lifeboat. A second later his board joined him.

'It's our job and we love doing it.'

'Thank you,' the surfer said. 'The weather changed so quickly.'

Thurza nodded and glanced up at the heavy sky. Not great weather for much, but to her the rain didn't matter, because the day was already perfect.

'Your mum contacted the station when you didn't arrive back on the beach at the time you'd agreed. You're safe now.'

'Th-thank you,' the boy stammered, just as a large wave hit the side of the boat, spraying them with water.

Thurza grinned and wrapped a blanket around the teenager. 'Best hold on. The way my boss drives this boat, the ride back may be a little rough and hairy.'

'I heard that,' her boss complained from where he steered the boat. 'Best we get back quick—in case Logan decides to leg it.'

Thurza laughed and shook her head, confident that her man was going to be exactly where she'd left him.

Returning her attention to the teenager, she crouched at his side and said, 'Congratulations. You're officially my fifth rescue.'

'Really?' the teenager asked.

Thurza nodded.

With Logan's support, she'd crushed her fears and was now a member of the town's lifeboat team. She loved the job and, although keeping the promise to her father was important, she had fulfilled her own dream.

Her colleague Fred pointed to the beach. 'Someone's keen.'

Thurza twisted round and searched the shore until she found Logan, her husband of less than two hours, patiently waiting, holding a twin in each arm. Dressed in a black tux and a sky blue shirt, Logan defined the word 'sexy'. The man owned his style and confidence, and his understanding smile as the boat returned to the station just topped off his gorgeousness.

She loved him. He and their sons were the reason she woke every morning and said thanks to the universe before she closed her eyes every night.

Climbing out of the boat, still in her all-weather gear, she waved to the other crew members and headed over to Logan. 'I'm so sorry.'

'Don't apologise,' Logan said. 'You stayed long enough to say *I do*. I asked for no more. It's legal and there's no backing out, Mrs Fox. You're finally my wife.'

An emergency call had come in seconds after the vicar had pronounced them husband and wife. A surfer in difficulty. And, as the newest member of the lifeboat team, Thurza had kissed Logan at the altar and then rushed off with several of their guests, still wearing her ivory wedding dress—which she now needed to change back into.

Logan handed over Axel, and then pulled Thurza close against him, circling his now free arm around her waist, not the slightest bit concerned about getting his clothes wet.

Her waist was slowly thickening, thanks to their new baby growing inside her. Soon their group of four would become five, and their happiness and excitement grew with each day. This time Logan would experience the pregnancy with her. This time he would be an involved expectant dad.

In the last few months their lives had changed in several ways. They'd moved into a new home and Logan had become a partner at the surgery where they both worked. Every plan they made concerned their long-term future. One they intended to share together. After so much time apart, fate had brought them back together, and they were determined to relish every precious moment.

'Have I told you how beautiful you are?' Logan asked.

Smiling brightly, she nodded. 'Yes—just before I rushed off and left you at the altar.'

'You returned, though.'

She brushed a hand over his cheek. 'I'll always come back to you, Logan,' she promised. 'You and the boys are home to me.'

He kissed her then, and the wolf whistles from her colleagues already on their way back to the reception and the meal that waited for them all didn't stop them from showing how much love flowed in their hearts.

Somehow, despite everything, fate had chosen to lead them back to each other, and this time they were going to stay together and make it work. Together as a family. Together as lovers. Together for always.

'Let's go and rejoin our guests. We've a married life to start enjoying.'

She smiled and kissed him once again, her heart full of love for the man who held her and for the two small boys resting on their hips. 'You say the best things, husband. You really do.'

* * * * *